*The End of Hell*

**MARK CARP**

To Michael,
All the best —
Always!

Mark Carp

*AuthorHouse*™
*1663 Liberty Drive, Suite 200*
*Bloomington, IN 47403*
*www.authorhouse.com*
*Phone: 1-800-839-8640*


© *2008 Mark Carp. All rights reserved.*

*No part of this book may be reproduced, stored in a retrieval system, or transmitted by any means without the written permission of the author.*

*First published by AuthorHouse     11/21/2008*

*ISBN: 978-1-4343-8053-1 (sc)*


*Library of Congress Control Number: 2008903640*

*Printed in the United States of America*
*Bloomington, Indiana*

*This book is printed on acid-free paper.*

War is hell in

more ways than

you can imagine.

*Mark Carp*

# DEDICATION

*To the men and women of the United States*

*Armed Forces who sacrificed so much*

*in time of war.*

ACKNOWLEDGMENTS

*I'd like to thank Arleen Grollman for typing the manuscript and Nancy Carp and Barbara Harr for reviewing it.*

## Chapter I

## *The Phone Call*

"Hello."

"Dad."

"Matthew, it's good to hear from you."

"How are things in sunny Florida?"

"So-so."

"Any problems?"

"Not exactly."

"Anything you want to talk to me about?"

"Not really."

"Are you keeping busy?"

"Not so much, lately."

"How about the card game?"

"I stopped going."

"Why?"

"Do you remember Maishie Cohen?"

"Maish Cohen? Maish Cohen? Oh yeah, the heavy one with corny jokes."

"Yeah."

"Wasn't he the one who smoked those stinking cigars?"

"He smoked a cigar that smelled so, that if the EPA had sat in on our card game, we would have been considered a bigger threat to the environment than global warming."

"So what about Maish Cohen?"

"He died."

"No."

"Yeah. I can't go back to the game and stare at an empty chair."

"I thought you couldn't stand him."

"Well, he was a friend, except for the cigars and jokes. It got so, I would say, 'For Christ's sake, Maish, deal the goddamn cards and stop with the Milton Berle jokes.' To tell you the truth, now that he's gone, I miss him like he was a brother."

"Are you still seeing that New York woman, Candice Schwartz?"

"Not so much, anymore."

"Why?"

"I think she was after my money."

"I thought she had money."

"Yeah, well, her money plus my money would equal a lot more money. When we went out, she'd spend money like I had a key to the United States Mint. I think she had angles. She was too sophisticated, if you know what I mean. So I kind of broke it off, at least for a while."

"So what do you do?"

"Oh, I sit by the pool and read the *Wall Street Journal* from cover to cover."

"And that keeps you busy?"

"Somewhat."

"Anything interesting?"

"I read some of these stories and get sick to my stomach."

"So why do you read the paper?"

"Because I've got time on my hands."

"Why do the stories make you sick?"

"The companies: One day they're taken private. Two years later they go public again, and it's the same company, while the promoters make all the money. Sometimes I think these firms are being guided by croupiers: Heads they win, tails you lose. It wasn't like that when I was in business."

"Dad, nothing stays the same."

"Yeah, but when we were in business, we made a product and were respected. Four Seasons Coats was a major label carried by the best stores. We didn't play numbers' games."

"Look, Dad, I got a letter from a Jewish war veterans' group which wants you to record your reflections from World War II."

"Why me? I was no hero."

"I guess they found out you were a combat soldier and were decorated."

"I wasn't John Wayne or even Audie Murphy. I was lucky I got back in one piece. You know if it weren't for your mother, I don't know if I could have adjusted to civilian life following the war. I was no damn good. She brought me back. We were married in 1947. That was a long time for two people to be together. I miss her terribly."

"Do you think you will want to cooperate with the veterans' group?"

"Yeah, I'll do it. I'll go to an electronics' superstore—the kind where the help can't help you and the personnel turn over by the week—buy a tape recorder and begin to talk. I hope the veterans will be satisfied with what they get."

"Dad, Iris and I will see you at the end of the month."

"I will finish my taping long before then."

"Dad, remember you're retired. Relax and enjoy life!"

"It's not so easy. Maybe I'm haunted by too many memories."

## Chapter II

## *England*

I bought an inexpensive tape recorder, a cassette, and began unleashing a torrent of memories that had long been suppressed.

"Testing, testing," I said into the recorder. I played the tape back and sounded okay. Frank Sinatra I wasn't, but I could be easily understood.

My name is David Kravitz.

The country has changed greatly since the eve of World War II. I remember that was a time of my first significant disillusionment. There was an anti-Semitic priest on national radio, Father Charles E. Coughlin, a real rabble-rouser and demagogue of the first degree. You would listen to his broadcasts and sit in fear. There was a Nazi Bund rally in 1939 at New York's Madison Square Garden, where the great Joe Louis fought. And, finally, there was Charles Lindbergh, my boyhood idol, a member of the America First Committee, who harbored anti-Semitic sympathies and had befriended Nazis. How could the "Lone Eagle" have been so stupid?

I entered the University of Maryland in September 1941 and on December 7, 1941, the Japanese attacked

Pearl Harbor. The country was soon in World War II against Japan, Germany and Italy.

I remember the stories and rumors of what was happening to Eastern European Jewry. I thought if these stories were only half true, this was barbarism beyond belief.

At the end of my sophomore year, I was drafted into the Army and went through basic training.

In 1944, I was in England, and we were preparing for the D-Day invasion.

That's when I first met Joe Moskowitz, a new man who joined our squad. We were taking a break during bayonet training, and he and I sat and began to talk.

"Where are you from?" he asked.

"Baltimore, Maryland."

"Did you go to college?"

"I finished my sophomore year at the University of Maryland and was drafted."

"Isn't that an agricultural college?"

"We're not farmers."

"What does your family do?"

"My father and grandfather are in the coat-manufacturing business. Four Seasons Coats is the name of their enterprise."

"Did you attend college, Joe?"

"I finished three semesters at City College of New York."

"Isn't that a school for socialists?"

"I guess in the way the University of Maryland is for farmers."

"Joe, what does your family do?"

"My father is a union organizer and my mother is an English teacher in Brooklyn, New York, where we live."

"What industries does your father try to organize?"

"He specializes in the clothing industry."

"Good," I laughed, "we're thousands of miles from home. I have one Jew in my squad and if my father knew his father, they'd probably try to shoot one another."

"David, we have our own war to fight."

"And survive," I added.

"L'chaim," (to life), he said.

On Saturday morning, Joe and I attended a Sabbath service and sat with Lieutenant Solomon Goldman, from St. Louis, Missouri, who headed our platoon. During the service, I didn't say a word.

As we returned to our barracks, Joe asked me about my reticence.

"Let's say I can't relate to prayer with the world in the shape it's in."

"Then why do you come?"

"It beats pulling duty on Saturday morning."

"They say there are no atheists in the foxholes."

"Is there room for loyal opposition?"

As Lieutenant Goldman walked with us, he asked Joe and me if we would be attending the USO dance that night.

We answered "yes."

"Lieutenant Goldman," I said, "you're becoming famous."

"How?"

"The story of you with the woman in London during the fire has made its way to headquarters."

"What story is that?" Joe asked.

"I was in a woman's apartment," Lieutenant Goldman said. "The woman's husband began knocking at the door.

"The woman said, 'It's my husband. He's very jealous. Hide in the trunk.' I did, and a fire started in the apartment building. I could hear people running to the door, carrying things with them. I stayed inside the trunk and yelled, 'Carry out the trunk. Don't forget the trunk.'"

I said, "I heard that story was told to General Patton."

"What did he do?" Joe asked.

"I heard," said the Lieutenant, "Patton said, 'A soldier like that ought to be court-martialed or be made General of the Armies. I'm not sure which.' Then he burst out in uncontrolled laughter."

"I hear at headquarters Lieutenant Goldman is referred to as Tyrone Manishevitz," I related.

"It would be a pleasure to live up to that title," Lieutenant Goldman said, smiling.

On Saturday night, Joe Moskowitz and I went to the USO dance, where the great Glenn Miller Orchestra played.

*The End of Hell*

I walked with Joe over to a group of women in uniform. I thought I recognized one, a Negro.

"Isabelle," I said, "what are you doing here?"

"I joined the WACs."

"What are the WACs?"

"We're the Women's Army Corps."

"Joe, I would like you to meet Isabelle Hudson."

"How do you do?" Then, after a pause, he said, "How do you two know one another?"

"My mother is a maid at the Kravitz house."

"Oh," Joe said, somewhat taken aback.

"Would you care to dance, Isabelle?" I said.

"Please."

I took her hand and escorted her to the dance floor.

"In the Mood," was playing. Isabelle was one helluva dancer: athletic, graceful and rhythmic. As they say, we really cut a rug.

Soon, members of my company began to stare at us. As I glanced over, I saw some of the southerners grow angry as Isabelle and I jitterbugged through the evening. I thought nothing of it.

The dance ended with the beautiful and melodic "Moonlight Serenade." Isabelle and I danced closely and I held her tightly, thinking wistfully of home and Pearl Segal, my girlfriend who attended Goucher College in Baltimore.

With the dance over, I gave Isabelle a hug and kissed her on the cheek.

As Joe and I were getting ready to leave, he said he had to go to the bathroom.

I told him I would wait for him outside.

Some of the southerners in the unit were waiting for me.

They said, "You cut a mean rug."

I smiled.

One said, "David, walk down the street with us, we want to show you something."

"Sure," I replied.

We walked, then I was pushed into an alley.

A distinctly angry southern voice rose up, "You nigger-loving Jew bastard."

Three of them jumped me and beat the hell out of me, while a fourth looked on in perverse delight.

Some twenty minutes later, Joe and Isabelle found me in the alley.

I was taken to a hospital where I spent the next four days. Fortunately, no bones were broken and I was able to recover quickly.

Lieutenant Goldman visited me in the hospital and after he spent time chatting with an attractive nurse, asked me how I felt.

"Okay," I replied.

"Kravitz, who did it?"

"It was Jones, Gomer, Crockett, and Sandwich looked on."

"It's too close to the time of invasion, so we won't take any formal action. We need all the men we have. So this will be hushed up, but I'll get even for you. Trust me."

"Yes, sir," I said and Lieutenant Goldman left.

Later that week, we had a major inspection. After our sergeant, Abner Peckinpaugh, finished, and we were dismissed, he said, "Kravitz, I want to speak to you."

"Yes, Sergeant."

"Kravitz, what happened to your horns?"

"Horns, Sergeant?"

"Yes, don't Jews have horns?"

I said, "The Army had them removed after I was drafted. The government is working on a regulation set, and they will be put in once the Army approves them."

"When will that be?"

"I hope any day, Sergeant."

I was then dismissed.

On Saturday morning, Joe Moskowitz and I attended services when we could.

After the service, the Jewish personnel would talk. It was a remarkable difference from the chit-chat in the barracks. There, getting laid and drunk were the two priorities of the day.

At shul, the discussions were largely intellectual. Everything was discussed, from history and religion to literature and philosophy, with some mathematics and who would win the American and National League pennants thrown in.

As D-Day approached, I began receiving less and less mail from Pearl Segal, which made me alarmed.

Joe said, to relieve my anxiety, "You know the mail is all screwed up, and on top of that it's censored, which ties it up more."

"I hope you're right."

"How long have you known Pearl?"

"We met in our senior year in high school at a party. Then we bumped into each other at a friend's house and began dating."

"What's her father do?"

"He's in the dress-manufacturing business."

"Hmmm, your father makes ladies' coats, her father makes dresses. It seems like a natural. Not only marriage but a merger."

"Not if her mother can help it."

"Why?"

"They're German Jews. We're Russian Jews. The German Jews have been in the country longer. They consider themselves more cultured. Mrs. Segal looks at us like we're shvartzers."

"I resent that term."

"I meant to use it as an analogy and not to be disparaging, Mr. Socially-Concerned."

"David, what is your idea of social justice?"

"In my house, justice is if you pay a man a dollar an hour, you better get two dollars an hour of production in return."

"Isn't that kind of limiting?"

"Not if you're looking to prosper."

We readied for the landing in France, where Joe and I would see our first combat action. He asked me if I thought about killing another human being. "If it's him or me, it better be him," I said.

He replied, he thought he'd "have a difficult time doing it."

"Joe, once they start shooting at you, I'm sure you'll feel differently. And remember, if we're captured by the Germans, get rid of the dog tags. We don't want to wear anything that's stamped 'Jew.' Also, remember when they look at you to see if you've been circumcised, tell them it's a common practice in America."

After a day's delay, we were lowered into a landing craft to make our way to Normandy Beach. As dawn broke, the armada was remarkable. There were ships everywhere. Lieutenant Goldman said to Sergeant Peckinpaugh, "I want to see the order of men in the landing craft."

"Sir, Kravitz and Moskowitz will be the first to exit."

"Sergeant, I'm making a change. I want Jones, Gomer, Crockett and Sandwich off the boat first. That's an order. If I find out you're disobeying me, you'll be the first casualty of D-Day. I'll personally see to it," he said as he held a pistol in his right hand.

"Yes, sir," replied Sergeant Peckinpaugh, sweating.

## Chapter III

*France*

We took our positions aboard the landing craft in the English Channel, and all of us were white with fear.

The water was rough and there was vomiting on the boat resulting from nerves and the choppy sea. I wish it would have been possible for the craft to turn back, possibly because of a malfunction. But such was not the case as we headed towards the German-held beaches of France.

As the door of the landing craft was lowered, we stepped into the channel and were chest deep in water. Joe and I were behind Jones, Gomer, Crockett and Sandwich. We began taking casualties. Jones and Crockett were killed and Sandwich was wounded severely and would die the next day. Gomer, Joe and I made it to shore uninjured as did Sergeant Peckinpaugh.

At that moment, I knew Joe and I had survived because Lieutenant Goldman had reversed the order of exit from the landing craft as a result of my being jumped by southerners because I was a Jew who danced with a Negro woman.

On Normandy Beach, there was tremendous disorganization and confusion. Sergeant Peckinpaugh did his best to assemble some squads under fire as our medics attended to the wounded.

We had to hold the beach and advance. This was one helluva introduction to war. If this was baptism by fire, I was surely baptized.

After being pinned down on the beach, we began to move forward.

I had survived my first brush with combat, as did Joe, scared, in awe but unhurt. I was thankful and lucky to be alive.

Soon we broke out of the beachhead and began to advance into Nazi-held France.

Our progress in France at first seemed rapid, then it was met by greater resistance. The combat was intense, and we took more casualties but kept advancing.

Joe and I quickly became hardened combat veterans. We tried to analyze things as best we could, kill or maim the Nazis and live to fight another day. War is a cruel, dirty business, which you have to learn to survive.

As we continued to advance, we began to encounter members of the French underground. Somehow, during the years of occupation, they were able to accumulate a vast cache of weapons. Sometimes they did the dirty work for us.

We entered a French town where German bodies were dumped into abandoned pits—no doubt the work of the underground. A man named Pierre met with Lieutenant Goldman and our company commander, Captain Joseph

Pierce, and gave them information on the Germans' whereabouts.

As a result of this intelligence, we found several squads of Germans who were preparing to eat breakfast. Our company surrounded them, opened fire and annihilated the group. Those who weren't killed surrendered hastily, perhaps happy they were alive and relieved the war was apparently over for them.

Several of our men escorted the Germans to the rear where they were interrogated as prisoners of war.

We returned to the town where Lieutenant Goldman and Captain Pierce met Pierre and talked at length with him, trying to obtain more information on German positions.

Following the meeting with Pierre, Lieutenant Goldman approached Joe and me.

"Yom Kippur services," he said, "are being held in Lunéville on Tuesday night and Wednesday."

The he read from a directive: "All personnel of the Jewish faith will be excused from duty in order that they may attend the Day of Atonement services."

"Isn't that town in German hands?" I protested.

"It is," said Lieutenant Goldman.

"I thought you repented on Yom Kippur, not committed suicide," I said.

"I'm sure the town will be secure by the time services are held," replied Goldman.

"And if we're attacked and run out of ammunition, should we throw the Torah at them," I said.

Ignoring my sarcasm, Joe said, "I'll be pleased to attend."

"How about you, Corporal Kravitz?" asked Goldman.

"I'll go, just make sure we have plenty of ammo."

Then, after thinking about the situation, I said, "You don't think the Army wants the Germans to notice a substantial amount of Jewish personnel is going into a synagogue so the building will draw fire and expose enemy positions that could be counterattacked by our forces?"

Lieutenant Goldman shrugged and Joe didn't comment.

"My God," I exclaimed, "we're being used as guinea pigs!"

"It can't be that bad," countered Goldman, "and I'll be attending."

Alluding to an Errol Flynn movie, "They Died with Their Boots On," I said, "I wonder if the sequel will be, 'I Died with a Prayer Book in My Hands.'"

Then I said, "If Lunéville is free of Germans, I'll go. My idea of Yom Kippur is not to watch the Nazis carry around the Torah."

By then, Goldman and Moskowitz were hysterical from my words, which I didn't intend to be funny.

As I looked at their faces, I said, "Because of this, I hope we aren't known as 'The Three Lunatics of Lunéville.'"

Goldman and Moskowitz continued laughing.

I said, "I never thought about surviving Yom Kippur services."

"I guess you never had my rabbi in St. Louis," said Goldman.

"At least you were safe," I replied.

"I'm not sure. When I had my final bar mitzvah rehearsal and made several mistakes, my rabbi hit me over the head. That man had a sledgehammer right!"

"I know now both of you are crazy," I said. "Your rabbi thinks he's Joe Louis, and we may have Nazis in shul. Jesus Christ, I'm fighting the goddamn Germans with two Jews who are nuts!"

## Chapter IV

## *Atoning in Lunéville*

Joe, Lieutenant Goldman and I made it to Lunéville, where, to my astonishment, there were some three hundred and fifty Jewish soldiers waiting to observe Yom Kippur, the Day of Atonement.

As I saw my fellow combatants, I felt a tremendous sense of pride. As the service was about to commence, I thought about being jumped in England because I was a Jew who danced with a Negro woman, and Sergeant Peckinpaugh and his slights. I could never understand whether Peckinpaugh was an anti-Semite or just incredibly ignorant. He had asked me where my horns were and why Moskowitz and I weren't writers for the *Stars and Stripes*.

I told him, I'm waiting for the regulation-Army horns and not to hold it against me because I finished two years of college and was "capable of writing in complete sentences since the sixth grade." He never seemed to grasp the intended sarcasm in my answers. Anyway, I was always amazed at who had positions of responsibility in the Army and how they got them.

As I saw the rabbi, Chaplain David Max Eichorn, mount the bemah, I thought about home, where my parents would be attending with my brother and, no doubt, Pearl Segal would be attending with her parents. I never felt such a sensation—it was a feeling of awe, irony and surrealism. Here I was an unrepentant killer, supposedly atoning, in part, for the unatonable, because it was kill or be killed.

During the service, as had become my custom, I didn't utter a word in protest over the condition of the world. However, both Joe and Lieutenant Goldman followed the Hebrew and English closely and spoke very good Hebrew which impressed me.

Joe was given an aliyah, which he performed perfectly, and on his way back to our row, was congratulated by a number of the congregants.

When I saw that, I became very emotional.

Up until my entrance into the Army, I led a fairly cloistered life. I was privileged and educated. I never thought of the Jews as a particularly intellectual people until I was exposed to everyone else. Then I understood, for the first time, there were differences.

At the conclusion of the service, I felt better than I had in a long time. But I soon became depressed as Joe, Lieutenant Goldman and I made our way back to the line—where there would undoubtedly be more fear and killing. What a world!

Soon after the service, I found out about a conversation Chaplain Eichorn had had with a lieutenant in intelligence.

The lieutenant thanked Rabbi Eichorn for his contribution to military intelligence.

*The End of Hell*

When the rabbi protested he didn't understand what the officer meant, the lieutenant said, "The Germans could not fail to observe the movement of American vehicles and men through the streets to the synagogue. If they had artillery at the edge of the forest, they would have been able to drop some shells through the roof of the synagogue. Since they did not do so, we now know that they have withdrawn their artillery to the middle of the forest. Simple, isn't it?"

"Yes," said Rabbi Eichorn, "but why didn't you tell me about this before the service?"

"Duty before friendship," said the intelligence officer. "Besides, Chaplain, if perchance you had refused to hold the service, I would not have found out what I wanted to know. And if I had told you and you still would have held the service, you might not have been able to concentrate sufficiently on your sermons and other rabbinical duties."

"Thanks for your kindly consideration of my spiritual welfare," said the Rabbi.

As I said, how certain people got positions of high responsibility in the Army was beyond me.

## Chapter V

## *Random Insanity*

I never got used to war. You exist in a world of random insanity. There are periods of boredom and moments of sheer horror. In battle, plans seem to disintegrate soon after the first shot is fired. You have to be lucky to survive.

We came under attack and a mortar shell exploded near me. Because of the conic shape of the blast, had I been three feet farther away, I would not be making this tape. But that is war and luck is an immeasurable part of survival.

The only man in my company I'm close with is Joe Moskowitz. It's unique how war can make a "brother" of the guy next to you. I decided I didn't need or want any more close relationships. Men are killed, wounded and replaced. Sometimes I wonder how the wounded feel who are no longer capable of fighting. One of our men, Sam Caruthers, had his leg amputated below the knee. Now he would be crippled for life, but at least he had survived. Some tradeoff: deformity for survival. In war, you think about these perverse calculations.

Letters from home are a temporary elixir from the conflict.

## The End of Hell

But the mail is uncertain and newer letters arrive sometimes before older ones. In one instance, my father wrote about Uncle Joe Gershovitz, who died. Later, I got a letter that he had been with Uncle Joe and how good he looked, in spite of a recent heart attack, and how he was optimistic about his chance for a complete recovery.

Some mail is as bad as the uncertainty of war. I saw a married man in our company receive a "Dear John" letter. Here was a guy in the middle of God-knows-what and his wife runs off with someone else. Like they say, war is hell but in more ways than you can imagine.

However, the mail I covet most are letters from Pearl Segal. Sometimes her letters are warm and make me want to rush home and hold her. Other times, they seem a bit formal and standoffish, making me wonder if she's seeing someone else.

Always, however, my letters to her express love and passion. Sometimes I surprise myself in my use of language. I guess that's what happens when you let your heart and emotions flow.

I often discuss my feelings about Pearl with Joe. After I received a formal, dispassionate letter from her, I said to him, "I bet her mother is working on her."

"Oh," he said.

"Yeah," I replied, "I can hear it now, 'Pearl, with your face and figure you should be seeing others.' Translation, you should be dating a young man with a nice German-Jewish name: Blumenfeld, or Eisenstein or Frankfurter. No names that end with itz or sky. A medical student from Johns Hopkins would be her speed, not a Russian Jew whose family started out as peddlers with a wagon and worked their way up from the streets to become large and respected coat manufacturers."

"So Pearl is a real shayner punim."

"Yes, except you can't use Yiddish in front of Mrs. Segal. I did once and she told me: 'We don't talk like that in our house.'"

"What's she ashamed of?" said Joe.

"You'll have to ask her."

"After the war," he joked. "Besides America does have a way of bridging differences. It is a melting point."

"If Mrs. Segal had a pot, she'd want me in it melting in boiling water."

Joe, too, shares his letters with me. In one, his father wrote him that there is a rumor that the Brooklyn Dodgers will be bringing in Negro players after the war.

I remarked, cynically, that maybe in his next letter he'll write a Jew will become Miss America.

It seemed to me Joe and his family could idealize anything. On the other hand, there were members of my family who were professional brooders, and never had anything good to say about anything. It was so bad with my mother's sister, Tessie, I swore she hadn't had a good day in forty years!

I remember once I asked her how she felt. Forty-five minutes later, I was still listening as she gave me an ache-by-ache account of her medical history.

Often Joe would intellectualize over matters and try to place things in a meaningful context. One day he began talking about the post-war order and the need for nations to unite in a league so as to maintain peace.

I said, "It was tried once with League of Nations and look where we are now."

"Just because it was tried once and failed doesn't mean it's a bad idea. Mankind must probe for ways that can best assure an era of peace."

Joe also foresaw an era of lessened anti-Semitism and equal rights for Negroes.

"As far as I'm concerned," I said, "I just hope if I get back that Father Coughlin will no longer be on the radio and the demagogues will cease to be as demagogic."

"Out here," he replied, "all I have is my idealism and belief. Hope helps me to keep going."

"That's fine, Joe, but don't forget to duck. In war, your ability to ponder the future is based on your ability to know when to keep your head down."

Joe acknowledged what I said and smiled.

## Chapter VI

## *The End of Virginity*

We were encamped outside of a small town in France, waiting to be resupplied.

The town, like most of the country, had suffered from Nazi occupation. Everything was now for sale, including the women.

I was propositioned by one during an evening in the town. At first, I misunderstood what she meant. Then I understood.

I decided to spend time with her that evening. It was my first experience, and I felt tense and awkward. She led me upstairs to a second-floor bedroom. As we began to undress, I was stunned as she removed her wig, exposing a shaved head, a punishment, no doubt, for having been a Nazi collaborator.

I thought to myself that maybe she had been an officer's kept woman and enjoyed the fruits of occupation as her countrymen suffered.

We were soon in bed and she was stimulating me. My orgasm occurred some ten minutes after I entered her bedroom. She and I got dressed. She donned her wig and went out to seek more business.

The sex was stimulating, but I would have preferred my first time to be romantic love with Pearl and not some Nazi collaborator who was forced to sell her body.

It's funny how the fortunes of war can change quickly, as her shaved head had indicated.

Back in camp, I told Joe about my experience. He was inquisitive. I went over the routine, and he kept peppering me with questions about how it felt. I said, "It's like masturbation, only better."

The next night, we went to the town and found the woman. It was now his turn. They went up to her second-floor bedroom and I waited. About twenty minutes later, he returned, smiling. He looked like a rooster about to crow.

"How was it?" I asked.

He answered me by broadening his smile.

"Maybe," I said, "when you return to New York, you can become a big Broadway producer and conduct your auditions on the 'casting couch.'"

"Not a bad idea," said Joe, still smiling.

"And I thought you wanted to live an intellectual life."

"That can wait," he said, laughing.

Word circulated in our company about my and Joe's exploits. The following day, Lieutenant Goldman approached Joe and me.

We told him the story of the French prostitute with the shaved head. That evening, the three of us went into town and inquired about whereabouts of the woman.

People were strangely silent and acted as if she never existed.

Joe and I were puzzled, and Lieutenant Goldman began to doubt our story. Finally, we bumped into a Frenchman who had a furtive look on his face.

We asked about the whereabouts of the woman. He took his finger and ran it across his throat. Then he went on to explain, "She exposed some members of a local French underground unit. The men and women were arrested and were never heard from again. The brother of one of the men who was arrested found her this morning." Then the Frenchman again ran his finger across his throat. After he did that, he turned and walked away, quickly disappearing from view.

The three of us tried to find him to get information on Nazi movements, but we were unable to locate him and returned to camp.

On the way, Joe said, "War reduces mankind to the state of animals, except we walk on two legs."

"Joe," I countered, "when they start firing at us, we can't even claim to be two-legged creatures because we slither along on our stomachs like snakes."

"The hell with you two philosophers," said Lieutenant Goldman, "all I wanted to do was get laid."

I said, "I forget Lieutenant Tyrone Manishevitz, you have a reputation to protect."

"Besides," Lieutenant Goldman laughed, "how does it look when an officer can't get laid and enlisted men can?"

"Grounds for court-martial," I volunteered, sarcastically.

"Maybe she has a sister," Joe laughed, "and your reputation can be salvaged."

"The way war goes," I said, "maybe they got her too."

## Chapter VII

## *On the Move, Again*

We've been resupplied and are on the move again. Members of our company have had a brief respite but remain war-weary, which causes mental fatigue, making me always feel tired.

Our next assignment is to attack a German position, entrenched on a hill. The task is formidable and the mission daunting. We began to stealthily move up the slope, maintaining silence. The enemy, too, is silent, creating an eerie atmosphere—one in which we expect the frightful quiet to soon be punctuated by the ominous intensity of weapons' fire.

Joe is next to me as we use a huge rock for cover. Our nerves are taut as we anticipate that the Germans will soon open up, exposing their positions.

"I wish the hell they would start firing," whispers Joe.

"Shhh," I say, trying to hear anything that might expose the Germans' whereabouts.

The silence remains deafening.

Suddenly, the Germans commence firing. Somehow we're on the side of an enemy machine-gun nest. The Germans don't see us. I have a clean shot at the gunner

*The End of Hell*

and pick him off. Then I get the soldier holding the ammo belt. As the remaining Germans hurriedly remove the two dead soldiers and start taking their positions, we move closer, and Joe hurls a hand grenade into the nest. Two Germans stagger out and Joe and I finish them off. We then move up to the nest and see three dead soldiers.

Our company is successful and we take the hill.

As the winter of 1944 approaches, we begin anticipating the Germans will try and stem the allied advance with a counterattack. The weather turns cold and on December 16, 1944, the Germans begin a massive counterattack which takes the American forces by surprise in its size and severity.

I remember during the battle how cold it was and that I thought my feet were frostbitten.

Our company is among those that is hardest hit. We begin to fall back. Sergeant Peckinpaugh asks for volunteers to stay up front to help direct artillery fire and provide cover while the others retreat.

I volunteer for the dangerous mission. Joe follows and our radioman, Sam Putnam, will stay and relay the coordinates to our artillery. As our troops fall back, there are five of us in position. If we're attacked by significant forces, we'll either be killed or captured.

I feel, however, in spite of the risks, we can complete the mission safely and successfully.

After a half hour, I'm able to sight a German position through binoculars. I give Putnam the coordinates and he relays the information to our artillery.

The first artillery barrage is beyond the German position. I make an adjustment to the coordinates and the next strike is short of the mark.

Finally, I take the average of the two coordinates and give Putnam a new reading. Now the artillery is hitting the mark and our mission is accomplished.

As we are about to retreat, we are attacked by a squad of Germans.

Our radioman is killed, but the four of us hold off the squad and are soon able to retreat, aided by the camouflage of night.

We are able to locate our company around midnight.

The next day Joe and I, along with the two other survivors, discuss the mission with Captain Pierce and Lieutenant Goldman.

Captain Pierce commends our valor and says we'll be recommended for Bronze Stars, including Putnam, posthumously, for "valor beyond the call of duty and demonstrating bravery under fire."

I thought the commendations were a bit exaggerated but didn't think any more of it.

Two days later, Sergeant Peckinpaugh approached Joe and me.

"You two," he said, "acted bravely." As Joe was about to thank him for the compliment, Peckinpaugh added, "for Jews."

Joe looked at me. I shrugged. Here I risk my life for this son-of-a-bitch, and I'm still a Jew.

*The End of Hell*

Oh, well, at least he didn't ask me when I would get my new set or horns. I guess our sergeant had too much on his mind and forgot.

The fighting—now known as the Battle of the Bulge—is bitter and intense. For two weeks I'm not sure whether the allies can repel the German offensive. Finally, the German's furious attack is repelled and we go back on the offensive.

Near the end of the battle, Sergeant Peckinpaugh and Captain Pierce are killed. I am promoted to sergeant and Lieutenant Goldman to captain, becoming the company commander.

The war has taken an emotional toll on me. I now don't care whether I live or die. When I tell Joe how I feel, he tries to rationalize things for me, explaining, "We've all been through hell but we'll get through this and make a better world and return to civilization and life as it's meant to be lived."

"How can you always be so high-minded?" I ask.

"Because without hope and ideals, you have nothing," he replied, with his usual sensitivity.

## Chapter VIII

## *Crossing the Rhine*

We crossed the Rhine River and entered Germany, where the fighting was fierce.

War is where life becomes cheap, civility virtually non-existent and inhibitions disappear. Men in our company begin to behave like animals—some don't give a damn about anything.

When we capture four German soldiers, I tell our men to take them back to headquarters for interrogation, some forty-five minutes behind the lines.

Some ten minutes later they return.

"What happened to the prisoners of war?" I ask.

"They tried to escape, Sergeant Kravitz," said a member of the detail. "So we shot them." I rolled my eyes.

Earlier, I saw our men wrap prisoners of war in barbed wire, shoot them and throw their bodies in the Rhine River.

At another point, we capture a German major. He was a large, barrel-chested man with an imperial mien and, even as a prisoner of war, exuded a sense of strength and forcefulness.

*The End of Hell*

He told me he would only surrender to an officer. I told the major, "You will surrender to me, Sergeant David Israel Kravitz of the United States Army."

He said, "I will not surrender to Juden scum," and spit in my face.

I took out a knife, slit his throat and killed him.

At that point, I was no damn good. A number of us, including Joe Moskowitz, were sent behind the lines for rest and relaxation and to gather ourselves. Joe, as usual, did his best to rationalize things. He talked about the world we were "helping to remake" and the "good we are doing."

I told him, "I don't need a lecture." Clearly, I had lost, as many of our men had, any sense of humanity.

The rest did us little emotional good, but it was good to get away from the stress of combat, at least for a few days. We soon rejoined our company.

Some three months after we crossed the Rhine, we captured Nuremberg.

In 1935, the Nuremberg Laws devested the Jews of their German citizenship and eliminated my co-religionists from civil-service positions.

Now it was a dead city, in ruins.

In an afternoon ceremony in Adolph Hitler Platz, a small American force was assembled, the National Anthem played and the Stars and Stripes raised.

We were addressed by Major General Wade H. Haislip. His opening words were: "We stand today amid the tumbled ruins of Nuremberg, amid the ruins of a city which gave its name to the infamous laws that violated every concept of human decency. Here Hitler reigned and strutted, and here he shouted at the multitudes of adoring Germans who used to gather in propaganda-filled" wonder. "In this city fascism flourished. We have conquered Nuremberg and we have destroyed it just as thoroughly as we shall destroy fascism and every evil thing connected with it."

While in Nuremberg, I found out I was awarded the Bronze Star for participating in a mission, along with Joe and three others, where we called in artillery fire over our heads and then held off German soldiers whose numbers were numerically superior to ours. Our radioman, Sam Putnam, was awarded his medal posthumously.

Captain Goldman, who succeeded Joseph Pierce as the company commander, pinned the medal on me and Joe in a brief ceremony along with the two others who survived the mission.

News of our decorations was published in the Baltimore newspapers. My father wrote how proud he was of me "fighting against the Nazis, the enemy of mankind, particularly our people, the Jews."

I also received an emotional letter from Pearl Segal. She said she was so proud of me and loved me. The letter at first buoys, but then depresses, me, as I realize even though a German defeat appears imminent, there is still more fighting to be done and more uncertainty lies ahead.

## Chapter IX

## *Dachau*

As I hold the microphone, my hands begin to shake. Nonetheless, I speak into it, saying: "We take the concentration camp at Dachau, twelve miles to the northwest of Munich."

Recalling the horrific sight of the day, I can no longer speak into the microphone. I turn off the tape recorder and begin to weep.

It seemed like only yesterday as I recalled the boxcars of Jewish dead in the Dachau railroad yard.

I cried then—a hardened combat soldier capable of killing a German major by slitting his throat and thinking nothing of it—and I cry now because of all the hell I saw and perpetrated, nothing affected me like the day I entered Dachau.

I tried to calm myself.

I paced in my condo unit, pounded a wall with an open hand, stepped onto my balcony, then came inside and paced some more. I felt like I was going to explode.

I decided to call Candice Schwartz to have someone to talk to.

She said, "David, you sound like you're having a breakdown. What's going on?"

"I'm doing a taping for a Jewish war veterans' group and as I recall these memories, I feel like I'm exploding."

"I didn't know you were in the war."

"Yes, too much so."

"How about if I come over and spend some time with you?"

"Please."

An hour later, Candice knocked on the door, entered and sat down on a sofa.

"David, how come you've stopped calling me?"

"Oh, I'm busy with this taping project."

"David, you look thin and drawn. Maybe you need a little nourishment. Let's go out and get something."

We were soon seated in a delicatessen-restaurant, and a large man came over with menus. His mien and walk reminded me of the German major whose throat I slit. I anticipated that he was going to call me "Juden scum." As he approached us with the menus, I held a sharp-edged table knife, ready to kill him if he would make such an utterance. My mind and emotions had taken me back to Germany.

As he came closer, my grip tightened.

Candice shrieked, "David, put that knife down."

Upon hearing those words, I dropped the knife and was immediately transmitted from the emotional upheaval of World War II Germany to Florida.

As the waiter put down the menus, I said, "Candice, let's leave."

"Okay," she replied.

The waiter was silent as we left the table.

"Candice, walk with me," I said.

"David, what triggered all this?"

"I was in Dachau."

"You were in a concentration camp?"

"I was among the liberators of Dachau."

"That was very heroic of you."

"I was no hero, just another dog-face trying to do his job and survive. Ever since that day, I knew I would never forgive those Nazi bastards for the evil they did."

"David, that was some fifty-five years ago."

"For me it will always be yesterday."

## Chapter X

## *Dachau Remembered*

I asked Candice to return to my condo while I would finish the episode on Dachau.

There was an eerie silence as I picked up the microphone to the tape recorder.

Rather than launch into a narrative chronology of the event, I said, "And for those who wish to stay in denial or say I exaggerated what I witnessed, let them call me or listen to this tape I'm about to make because I'll be a witness until the day I die.

"And may this tape bear witness after I'm gone."

I stopped the tape recorder and looked at Candice. She said, "David, you're doing the right thing. It's all right."

I nodded, turned on the tape recorder and began to speak. As I spoke, Candice began to weep.

I said: There were thirty-nine boxcars loaded with the Jewish dead of Dachau. We saw the killing machines: the gas chambers and crematoria.

Upon the liberation, we saw former inmates hunt down their guards, many of whom were now hiding in the camp.

The hunters had become the hunted.

## The End of Hell

As the guards were found, the former inmates beat them to death so savagely, their bodies were mutilated.

We saw the barracks of the inmates. They were filthy and lice-ridden.

As Joe and I toured the facility, we let our observations tell us the story. There was no need for words or interpretation of the hell we saw.

When the liberated of Dachau were suddenly able to get normal food, their bodies could not accept it and some died as a result.

Ironically, for their own protection, the former Jewish prisoners had to be forcibly detained in Dachau by the Americans so as to get the necessary medical attention and the proper amounts of nutrition their bodies could accept. As a newly liberated people, the former inmates had trouble accepting a new form of detention, even when it was done for their own good.

Joe and I remained numb from the sights and sounds we saw and heard.

On Saturday, May 5, Joe, who had recently been promoted to sergeant, and I were to attend a Sabbath service. The service was to be held in the main square of the Dachau compound at 10 a.m.

However, when a group of non-Jewish Polish inmates threatened that if the service were held they would break it up by force, the service was moved into a camp laundry.

This was another anti-Semitic slap, the kind I endured throughout the war. If it wasn't Sergeant Peckinpaugh asking me where my horns were, or my being jumped by the southerners in my company while they called me a nigger-loving Jew, it was when Joe and I walked together near some members of our company and one would say to another, loud enough so we could hear, 'Did you hear they changed the name of Roosevelt's New Deal to the Jew Deal?' or 'The Jew bankers got us into this war. It's because of the Jews that we're here.' Then there was the Jewish sneeze: 'Ha-Jew.'

Once I stopped and was ready to have it out with the sons-of-bitches when Joe pushed me forward and said, "Keep walking. You can't dignify fools."

So, because of the Polish threats, the service was now being held in a laundry, where only about eighty people could squeeze into the facility. Joe, Captain Goldman and I watched the service, that was attended by the former Jewish inmates, through an open window in the laundry. I was deeply moved and wept uncontrollably as I heard the Hebrew prayers. In some way, I wanted to grab the son-of-a-bitch anti-Semites I met and say, 'Look at this, you bastards, this is who we are, no matter what. No matter what they do to us, what they say to us, this is what we are.'

As the service was in progress, the famous Hollywood film maker, George Stevens, who made "Gunga Din" and had done movies with Fred Astaire and Ginger Rogers, entered the laundry. He was in charge of a Signal Corps unit, which was making the official Army pictures of Dachau, and had been prepared to film the service in the square. He asked Rabbi David Eichorn, the rabbi who conducted the Yom Kippur service in Lunéville, France, that Joe, Captain Goldman and I attended, and who was leading this service, why the service had been moved to the laundry. Rabbi Eichorn stopped davening to tell him he would give him the reason after the service.

Stevens waited outside the laundry. At the end of the service, Rabbi Eichorn explained why the service had been moved.

Stevens was irate. "I did not give up a good job in the movie business in Hollywood," he said, "to risk my life in combat for months and months in order to free the world from the threat of fascism and then stand idly by while the very victims of fascism seek to perpetuate its evils. I am going to do something about this."

Rabbi Eichorn and Stevens went to see the camp commandant, who was sympathetic to their views, and the service was scheduled the following day. It was to be held in the main square under the protection of the American military.

That Saturday night, Rabbi Eichorn took two hours to teach fifteen Hungarian Jewish girls the Irving Berlin masterpiece "God Bless America," which was to be sung at the service. Prior to that, the girls didn't know any English.

The next morning, Sunday, May 6, 1945, at 10 a.m., the service was held. It was attended by every Jewish male and female whose health permitted. In all, there were some two thousand Jews and non-Jews present. Multiple nationalities were represented at the event with flags and delegations. The service was ringed by the American military who stood with their backs towards us with fixed bayonets and loaded rifles to protect the participants.

As the service commenced, it was filmed by Stevens and his crew. The three of us, Captain Goldman, Sergeant Moskowitz and I, took part in the moving, surreal atmosphere. I began praying loudly, which must have seemed quite odd to Joe because, although I attended services during the war, I never said a word.

When Joe asked me why, I would say, 'I could not pray to God in a God-forsaken world.'

But today I was audible above everyone else. Following the service, Joe asked me why I prayed so loudly.

I said, "I wanted every Nazi bastard on earth and in Hell to hear me."

Joe issued a faint smile.

Then I put my hands on his shoulders and said, "Joe, I love you. If we get through the next remaining days, I hope I never see you again. Even though you are as close to me as anyone I've ever known, if I see you again, it will remind me of the hell we've all been through, and I never want to be reminded of this again."

Joe said, as I walked away, "No, David, this is the end of hell."

At that moment, I heard a rifle fire and dove to the ground. I, and other soldiers near us, stayed on the ground for some forty seconds. Then we rose slowly.

I looked at Joe. He didn't move. He was shot in the head. I yelled for the medics. One came. Joe was dead.

*The End of Hell*

A patrol was organized, led by Captain Goldman. I was in it and we totaled ten men.

Twenty minutes after Joe was killed, we were outside Dachau looking for a sniper. After patrolling for half an hour, I spotted a lone German soldier. I aimed and fired. He dropped. I ran to where he was. By the time I got there, he was dead. He was a young blonde, probably not yet seventeen. I knelt beside the young man, feeling overwhelmed by the loss of Joe, and realizing what this war had come to: People barely old enough to vote killing teenagers. I knew of all the absurdities man had conjured up, war was, by far, the most egregious.

The day after Joe died, May 7, 1945, Germany surrendered.

I put the microphone down and stared at Candice.

Candice, with tears streaming down her face and a stunned, bewildered look like nothing I had ever seen before, said, "David, I had no idea."

"I wish I didn't either," I replied.

I shut the tape recorder off and began staring at the ceiling, perplexed now as I was then.

Candice, still with a stunned look on her face, became hysterical but refused to tell me why.

Then she left my apartment, still hysterical.

## Chapter XI

## *Homeward Bound*

The following day, without Candice present, I began recording again.

In September 1945, I was on a large troop carrier, heading home.

While walking on the deck, I was approached by Chaplain Jonathan Taub, a rabbi who had been at Dachau with Chaplain Rabbi David Eichorn.

Knowing that Joe Moskowitz and I went from D-Day to Dachau together, and realizing how close we were, Rabbi Taub asked me, "Is there anything I could do to help preserve Joe's memory and accomplishments for his family?"

"Tell them," I said, "he was a good soldier and a better human being, and I can't say that about too many of the men I've served with."

"What's your immediate future, Sergeant Kravitz?"

"I don't know, Rabbi. I have two years of college to finish, but I don't know if I'll return. After going through this, I don't know if I could feel comfortable among college students."

"Sergeant Kravitz, education is a wonderful thing."

*The End of Hell*

"Rabbi, for the last two years, I've received the most remarkable education of all."

"In some ways we all have, and I'm sure it will be something we'll never forget."

"Not soon, anyway," I answered.

At that moment, Rabbi Taub excused himself to attend to some matters on board.

I stared over the side of the ship, looking at the infinity of the ocean, and thinking. We would be in New York in a few days. My family was to meet me as was Pearl Segal.

However, I worried that she wouldn't be there, as her most recent letters seemed detached and remote.

Still, I longed to see her.

As the boat entered New York Harbor and the Statue of Liberty came into view, I recalled the words by the Jewish poet Emma Lazarus, who wrote "The New Colossus," the poem placed at the pedestal of the monument.

I always recall this stanza: "Give me your tired, your poor, your huddled masses yearning to breathe free, The wretched refuse of your teeming shore. Send these, the homeless, tempest-tost to me."

After all, my grandfather, immediately prior to the turn of the twentieth century, steamed with his family into New York Harbor to make a new life away from the Russian czars and pogroms. Now I was returning after another score, affecting the Jews, was settled.

When would it stop: Pogrom, Holocaust, Religious Genocide, Unbound Insanity?

As the boat docked, I made my way down the gang plank with my duffel bag slung over my shoulder, desperately trying to locate my family and Pearl.

I put the microphone down and turned off the tape recorder. My recording was finished.

## Chapter XII

## *Family Matters*

My son Matthew and daughter-in-law Iris were visiting me in Florida.

"When is my grandson's graduation?" I asked.

"Josh graduates in May 2000 from the Columbia University Law School," Matthew said.

"Mazel tov," I said.

"Dad, did you finish your taping for the Jewish war veterans' group?" asked Matthew.

"Yes."

"Were you a big hero?" my son said, laughing.

"No, just a lucky survivor."

"I understand."

"You would have understood better had you gone through it. Thank God you didn't."

After a pause, I said, "How is my granddaughter Susan? Is she seeing anyone?"

"Who knows?" replied Iris. "She's independent. She has her friends. We don't ask and she doesn't tell."

"I see."

"When will you return to Baltimore?" Matthew asked.

"About April 1."

At that moment, there was a knock on the door.

"Excuse me," I said.

"Candice, what a pleasant surprise," I said as I opened the door.

She came into the living room and the four of us sat together.

"Candice," I said, "you remember my son Matthew and daughter-in-law Iris."

"Sure."

"You're all looking well," Candice said.

"It must be that I have my father's genes," Matthew said.

"I knew I was good for something," I replied. "Maybe if there is reincarnation, I'll come back as a horse. After my racing days are over, I'll be put out to stud."

Iris said, "Dad, I see you still have your crazy sense of humor."

"Laughter is good," I replied, "it helps you maneuver through the valleys of life and supplies a little perspective. Sometimes we all need perspective."

"Yes," Candice said, "especially as you age."

"Thirty nine isn't old," said Matthew.

Candice, looking at Iris, said, "When did you find out you married into a family of comedians?"

"Let me see... I think it was when I said 'I do.'"

"Why did it take you so long?" replied Candice sarcastically.

"At first I didn't understand when Matthew was joking," replied Iris. "To tell you the truth, I thought he was a little crazy."

"Like father, like son," I laughed.

At that point, we decided to go out for a bite to eat. We went to the same restaurant Candice and I were in when I saw the waiter who reminded me of the German major whose throat I slit.

That same waiter brought over the menus to our table. Apparently remembering when Candice and I got up to leave without ordering, he did a double take.

When my son saw that, he asked, "What's wrong with him?"

"Oh," Candice interrupted, "when your father was taping his World War II memoirs, he had begun recalling his experience in Dachau. It took a lot out of him. He was so upset, he and I left the restaurant without ordering."

"What is Dachau?" Iris asked.

"A concentration camp," Candice replied.

"Dad, you were in a concentration camp?"

"No, I was a liberator."

"What was it like?" Iris asked.

"I can't go into it again. It's too difficult. Maybe you can get the tape from the Jewish war veterans' group and listen. I feel like I never want to speak of it again."

"I see," replied Iris somberly.

At that moment, the waiter came over to take our orders.

"Excuse me," I said, and I got up and walked outside. Candice followed as did my son and daughter-in-law.

The waiter muttered, as he collected the menus, "I waited on this guy twice and have yet to serve any food or get a tip."

Now outside, Matthew asked, "Dad, are you okay?"

"I'm okay, let's return home."

"I'll serve something at the condo," Candice said.

"I'll help," said Iris.

We were soon having lunch in my condo.

I finished my sandwich quickly and said, "I'm sorry if I spoiled your afternoon."

"You didn't spoil anything, Dad," Iris said.

"You always say the right thing, Iris," I replied.

The four of us sat and began to talk quietly.

About an hour later, as Matthew and Iris were about to leave, I said, "In May my grandson Josh graduates from the Columbia University Law School, I'd like for you to attend with me, Candice."

"I'd love to go."

As Iris and Matthew walked towards the elevator, she asked, "Is your father okay?"

"He's always been like that," said Matthew. "He's an intensely personal man and sometimes he lets his feelings get the best of him. When he does that, he knows he's not good company."

"I see," said Iris.

In the condo, Candice asked me, "Why did you ask me to attend your grandson's law school graduation?"

*The End of Hell*

"I want to be with you, and I want to show you a museum in the Battery area of New York. It's dedicated to the Holocaust."

"Haven't you been tortured enough?"

"You have to see this."

"Okay."

## Chapter XIII

## *Memories and Graduation*

Candice and I attended my grandson Josh's graduation from the Columbia University Law School along with my son Matthew, daughter-in-law Iris and Josh's younger sister, Susan.

That night we had a celebratory dinner at a posh Manhattan restaurant and attended a Broadway show.

Josh had already landed a job with a law firm and when he told me his starting salary, I was floored.

"Can I have a loan?" I asked.

"Grandpa, all you have to do is ask," he said. But, he added, jokingly, "I'll have to run a credit report."

Oy, I thought to myself, one day out of law school and he's already thinking like a momzer lawyer.

The next morning, Candice and I met my family for breakfast in the coffee shop of our mid-town hotel. I told them I wanted to see the Museum of Jewish Heritage in the Battery area of Manhattan. We all agreed to go and to take two cabs. Candice, Josh and I rode in one, and Susan, Matthew and Iris in the other.

We toured the facility and as a group were quite taken with the exhibitions dedicated to the Holocaust. All of us became openly emotional as we walked through the architecturally striking museum.

We stood by a window and looked out at Ellis Island and the Statue of Liberty, making me recall how I felt when I entered New York harbor following my combat duty during World War II.

Next I went over to a screen to view a video tape of an event in which I had participated. It was the religious service in the Dachau concentration camp that was held on May 6, 1945.

I pressed a button, sat down and the tape played. There was Rabbi Eichorn leading the service. Inexplicably, I began to sing along as Rabbi Eichorn chanted the Hebrew prayers.

Josh turned to my son and said, "I never heard Grandpa speak Hebrew except when Bubbe Pearl died and he said Kaddish."

"You don't know the half of it," my son said. "Your grandmother, my mother, Pearl Segal Kravitz, aleha ha-shalom, was the Jewish angel. Following World War II, your grandfather had a difficult time adjusting. He thought people were trying to kill him on the streets of Baltimore, and once was found sleeping naked on the front lawn at 6 a.m. He never knew how he got there. It was my mother's love and patience that got him through that period and brought him back. Without her, I don't know if he would have made it."

Josh and Susan listened as their grandparents suddenly took on new identities.

Meanwhile, I kept replaying the tape, mesmerized.

Matthew put his hand on my shoulder and asked, "Dad, are you okay?"

"I'm okay," I said. "I had to see this. I was there fifty-five years ago at that service in the Dachau concentration camp. Being there was probably the most profound moment of my life. It all seems impossible now, but it happened."

We left that section of the museum and headed for the exit.

I said, "I want to go to Brooklyn."

"Brooklyn?" my son asked.

"Yes," I said.

"Why?"

"I want to see where he lived."

"Who's he?"

"Joe Moskowitz. He was a man I went through the war with. He didn't make it. He was shot dead by a sniper immediately after the conclusion of the service you witnessed. We were as close as brothers. You know the last words I said to him were words I should never have spoken."

"What were they?" my son asked.

"I told him, 'Joe, I love you. If we get through the next remaining days, I hope I never see you again. Even though you are as close to me as anyone I've ever known, if I see you again, it will remind me of the hell we've all been through, and I never want to be reminded of this again.'

"Then Joe replied, as I walked away, 'No, David, this is the end of hell.'

"Seconds later, he was killed by a sniper."

"My God," Matthew exclaimed.

I looked at Candice, whose eyes turned piercing as she stared at me while apparently hanging on every word. As I studied her face, she seemed to have a remarkable connection with the story. I also remembered how, when I taped this segment of my military remembrances for the Jewish war veterans' group, she ran out of my condo, hysterical.

"You know," I continued, "the service that was filmed was to be held the day before in the square at Dachau, but it had to be moved to a laundry because the non-Jewish Polish inmates threatened that if the service were held, they would break it up by force.

"I know if the service were held when it was scheduled, Joe would have lived.

"I've never felt a greater sense of frustration over any other turn of events, and God-forbid I should.

"As it was, when the service was held in the square, the some two thousand worshipers—Jews and non-Jews alike—were protected by the American military, who ringed the participants with their backs towards us and bayonets drawn in the event of trouble."

"Dad, did they ever get the sniper?" Matthew asked.

"We immediately went on patrol," I said. "I spotted a German soldier standing alone and shot him. By the time I got to his body, he lay dead. I stared into his open eyes. Then I studied his face. I don't think he was even seventeen years old. The next day Germany surrendered.

"Some days I'm haunted by that young German's face. Killing never bothered me until the day Joe died and I killed that German boy.

"Even when I killed up close, it didn't disturb me. Once we captured a German major and he said he would only surrender to an officer.

"I said, 'You'll surrender to me, Sergeant David Israel Kravitz of the United States Army.'

"He said, 'I won't surrender to Juden scum,' and he spit in my face. Then I took out a knife, slit his throat and killed him.

"I did that without remorse, emotion, shame, or conscience.

"But killing that boy that day still bothers me."

"Dad," my son said, "you weren't much older than he was."

"When I killed him, I thought to myself: This war had come to people barely old enough to vote killing teenagers."

Again I stared at Candice who seemed to remain morbidly attached to my words—more as an emotionally connected participant than as a listener.

When we were outside the museum, my son and daughter-in-law said they would return to the hotel, while Candice, Susan, Josh and I took a cab to Brooklyn to see where the Moskowitz family lived during World War II.

## Chapter XIV

## *Finding Ghosts*

I gave the cab driver the address of where the Moskowitz family lived during World War II.

There was silence in the cab as we drove over the Brooklyn Bridge.

I saw a sign for Nathan's of Coney Island. I laughed to myself because Joe always told me how good those hot dogs were.

We soon pulled up in front of the former Moskowitz family residence. It was in a run-down area of Brooklyn, and the apartment building was in very poor condition. Candice seemed to know precisely where we were, but I didn't ask her why.

The four of us left the cab and walked up and down the block where the residence was.

After a few minutes, we returned to the cab. Candice then gave the driver directions. We stopped about eight blocks away at a dilapidated playground. It contained a basketball court and some handball courts. A basketball rim dangled loosely from the base of the backboard, held up by some metal strips which prevented it from falling to the ground. Parts of the metal fence were torn away, and along the fence line, I saw needles. There was graffiti splattered on a concrete wall and the paving on the courts was torn up. The playground was barely usable. I walked over to a sign which also had graffiti on it. The sign read: Sergeant Joseph L. Moskowitz Memorial Playground.

I walked over to Candice. "How did you know this playground was here?" I asked her.

"Joe was my oldest brother."

"What?"

"Yes."

Candice went on to explain, "There was a ten-year age difference between us. When Joe went off to war and was stationed in England, I was nine years old. We remembered his letters and how upbeat they were, full of energy and optimism.

"As the war was about to end, we thought surely he was coming back. Then we got a knock on the door. It was a U.S. Army sergeant who gave the news to my parents. We sat shivah and a flag with a gold star was hung on our window.

"Joe's death nearly killed my father. When Joe died, things were never the same.

"I saw what his death did to my parents. I prayed to God every night to bring him back. I thought if God could deliver us from Egyptian bondage and divide the Red Sea, He could surely bring back Joe.

"I remember walking to a synagogue a few blocks from where we lived and talking to the rabbi. I asked him if he could talk to God about bringing back Joe."

"What did he say?"

"He said, 'God's ways are often not understood. One day he may return but in an image that may be hard for you to understand.'

"I soon realized Joe would never be back. But at least for a while I had what Joe always had—hope."

There was a sign on the fence saying a fundraising campaign had commenced to restore the playground. I wrote down the phone number. The four of us were soon in the cab, returning to our midtown-Manhattan hotel.

On the return trip, Candice asked Susan about her career.

"I'm in advertising," she said.

"Susan also writes poetry," I added. "She is very skillful. Her work reminds me of the poetry my wife Pearl used to write. It's full of sensitivity and meaning, with a beautifully rhythmic flow."

"Grandpa, you're embarrassing me."

"And," I said, "it's my greatest pleasure to do so."

When we returned to the hotel, I called the number on the sign and made an appointment for late the next morning to meet Sidney Cohen, who was in charge of the fundraising campaign.

That morning Candice and I had breakfast with Matthew, Iris, Susan and Josh, all of whom were returning to Baltimore.

Candice and I entered a cab to return to Brooklyn for our appointment. We came to Mr. Cohen's office, and he met with us promptly.

We introduced ourselves and I told him I had served in World War II with Joe. Candice explained she was Joe's younger sister.

Mr. Cohen did a double take and said, uncomfortably, "I didn't know he had a sister."

To avoid any embarrassment, I said may I see the plans for the refurbished playground and construction budget.

Mr. Cohen, while still staring at Candice, handed me the requested materials. As I opened the plans, I saw drawings for the refurbished basketball and handball courts, a new fence and a team house to be built. I then saw the construction and annual budget, which provided for a full-time playground director.

"I want to assist in the fundraising," I said. "I'm tired of lying down in Florida, bored stiff. I want to be useful again."

As I stared at the construction plans, I said, "There are a number of organizations we can approach for money. I don't know why we can't raise the money in six months and have the playground operable in September 2001, by the time the kids return to school."

"That's very kind of you, Mr. Kravitz," Cohen said.

"Call me David."

"And you call me Sid."

"I'm going to make a contribution."

I wrote the amount on a slip of paper and handed it to Sid.

"David," he said, "that's very generous of you."

I then looked at Candice and she agreed to a significant contribution.

Sid then said, "I want you to get in touch with Eddie Moskowitz."

"Who's Eddie Moskowitz?" I asked.

"He's a rabbi in Brooklyn," he replied.

"Was he some kind of family relative?" I asked.

"He's my brother," Candice said.

## Chapter XV

## *Ghosts Revisited*

At breakfast the next morning, I asked Candice why she had never mentioned her brother, Eddie.

"I haven't seen him in eight years," she said. "Eddie and Joe were closer in age—only four years apart. When Joe died, it was Eddie who did his best to hold the family together. He had the sensitivities of Joe and my father. And Eddie was a fighter.

"I knew when Joe died, my world had changed and, even at a young age, I wanted to 'escape.' I wanted to leave Brooklyn and a household of sorrow behind. When I was eighteen and had graduated high school, I left Brooklyn and landed a job in Manhattan, where I lived. I was young and attractive.

"I worked in a publishing house, attended college at night, and eventually rose to an associate-editor position. I began to socialize and developed a circle of friends, who were urbane and sophisticated.

"It's funny, though I lived over the bridge from Brooklyn, I might as well have been on another planet.

"In my middle twenties, I met Alan Schwartz, a divorced investment banker who was ten years my senior. He had two children from his previous marriage. We had a daughter, who lives in Manhattan and is divorced with a daughter of her own. Alan died five years ago and left me well provided for."

"Are you close with your daughter?"

"Not like I should be."

"Now tell me about Eddie."

"Everyone confronts adversity differently. When Joe died and the atmosphere grew depressing in our house, my impulse was to retreat from that reality and find solace, somehow, some way. So I left Brooklyn.

"Eddie, on the other hand, sought to explore the world of religion and the soul. He became a rabbi. He was at first an associate rabbi; then he became a rabbi at the same congregation in Brooklyn. When Brooklyn began to change racially and many of the congregants moved away, Eddie made it his personal crusade to keep his synagogue going.

"So you see his character is different from mine: He stayed and fought while I ran.

"The thing that maybe he appreciated most after Joe died was when Rabbi Taub, who had been at Dachau, came to visit and told us one of the men with whom I returned on ship to the United States said, 'Tell the family, Joe was a good soldier and a better human being.' I knew how much those words were appreciated by Eddie, my mother and father."

"Candice, I said those words."

"I suspected you did, that's why I brought them up."

"Is having this talk hard for you?"

"No. It's almost a confession—I'm baring my soul so you can see who and what I am. If I had to do it all over again, I would have done things differently. But when tragedy occurred, I wasn't ready or able to be strong."

"Candice, I'm going to call Eddie about the fundraising effort."

"Okay."

That night she and I had a quiet dinner and took in a movie.

The next morning I called Eddie at his synagogue and made an appointment to see him. As we were about to enter the cab, Candice changed her mind and decided not to go.

"You're going," I said.

I took her hand and we entered the cab.

She began to cry.

"Are you okay?"

"I just needed to cry. Maybe I needed to cry like this years ago. Maybe I've never been honest with myself or my emotions."

As the cab sped towards Brooklyn, I said, "Today you can get in touch with part of a past you avoided. Repentance is good for the soul."

"And necessary," Candice added.

The cab let us off in front of Eddie's synagogue. I rang the doorbell. Eddie met us at the door.

"Hello, Candice," he said stiffly.

"Hello, Edward."

*The End of Hell*

Then she reached out and hugged him. Both had tears in their eyes. The unspoken wall that had existed between them seemed to disappear. On seeing their reunion, I, too, became emotional.

A few minutes later, after all of us gained our emotional composure, we sat in Eddie's office. He told us that roughly ten percent of the monies needed for the playground redevelopment and construction of the team house had been committed. He then took out from a desk drawer a list of organizations that were to be contacted.

He made a copy of the list for me. On it were Jewish war veterans' groups, B'nai B'rith lodges, charitable foundations and Hadassah groups, in New York, Connecticut and in Northern New Jersey. Eddie also gave me a copy of a speech he used along with a slide presentation. He said he would provide Candice and me a projector.

We began to divide up the names on the potential donor list. I felt energized, committed and happy to be putting my ample free time to productive use again.

Eddie turned, faced me and said, "It was hard for me to imagine Joe as a combat soldier."

"You know before we went into combat, he said to me he thought it would be hard for him 'to take another man's life.'"

"I can hear him saying that," said Eddie.

"Anyway," I said, "'when we go into combat and they're shooting at you, I'm sure you'll feel differently.'

"And, of course, he did. Joe was tough. It was an honor to share a foxhole with him. He was a hard-nosed bastard, if you don't mind my using that word in your synagogue."

"It's okay and I appreciate what you're telling me."

"You know," I went on, "he wasn't awarded the Bronze Star because he was a slacker."

"Joe," Eddie said, "always wrote us about a Jewish guy from Baltimore who went to services but never prayed because he was upset with the conditions of the world. I assume that was you."

"It indubitably was."

"And how are you about religious matters today?"

"I saw war. I witnessed Dachau. I'm still troubled."

"Tell me about Dachau and what happened to Joe."

"Dachau was hell on earth. It was literally the poster child for the lunacy of Nazism.

"The service that was filmed, the one after which Joe was shot, was actually supposed to be held the day before in the square at Dachau.

"When the former Polish inmates threatened to disrupt the event if it was held in the square, it was moved to the laundry.

"George Stevens, who made 'Gunga Din' and did movies with Fred Astaire and Ginger Rogers, was to film the service in the square. When he found it was moved to a laundry, where only eighty people could attend, he came in during the service and asked Rabbi David Eichorn, who was conducting the service, why it had been moved.

"Following the service, Rabbi Eichorn explained the reason for the move. Then Stevens and Rabbi Eichorn visited the camp commandant. The service was held the next day, May 6 at 10 a.m. Two thousand people attended, both Jews and non-Jews alike. The American military ringed the service with their bayonets fixed and their backs towards the worshipers for protection.

"The night before, fifteen Hungarian Jewish girls, who had never spoken a word of English, were taught 'God Bless America,' which they sung at the service.

"That day I practically shouted out the prayers, the first time I prayed out loud during the war. When Joe asked me why, I said, 'I wanted every Nazi bastard on earth and in Hell to hear me.'

"I remembered Joe smiled at me faintly.

"Then I put my hands on his shoulders and said, 'Joe, I love you. If we get through the next remaining days, I hope I never see you again. Even though you are as close to me as anyone I've ever known, if I see you again, it will remind me of the hell we've all been through, and I never want to be reminded of this again.'

"Joe said, as I walked away, 'No, David, this is the end of hell.'

"Then Joe was shot and killed by a sniper.

"We immediately organized a patrol. I spotted a lone German and shot him. As I went over to his dead body, I saw he probably wasn't seventeen.

"The war ended the next day.

"Sometimes I'm still haunted by the youth of that German boy's face. But that's war in all its horrible 'glory.'"

Eddie interrupted my story to say, "Joe understood you didn't mean what you said about never seeing him again."

"Rabbi, I did mean it. Oh, in time I would have gotten over it and we would have gotten together. But at that time I never felt so strongly about anything in my life."

"Joe understood that," repeated Eddie.

"I know he did. I wish I hadn't said it, but I had to."

"I understand," said Eddie.

As Candice and I left Eddie's synagogue, she said, "When I was a little girl and went to see the rabbi to ask him to bring Joe back, he said, 'God's ways are often not understood. One day Joe may return in an image that may be hard for you to understand.'

"Now here you are. I love you, David."

"Candice," I said, "belief is about what you believe in."

"And how about you, David?"

"Like I say, belief is about what one believes."

"And you?" she repeated emphatically.

"I'm not sure about anything, although I'd like to tell you otherwise."

Because Candice had been spending nearly all her time in Florida and leased her co-op apartment, she and

*The End of Hell*

I would have to find a place to live. We spent the next several days looking. When we found a furnished unit we liked and the agent told us the monthly rental, I said, "I'm only renting it, not buying it."

The agent replied, "Maybe you should look elsewhere."

"No," I said, "I'll take it. I'll sign a six-month lease with a six-month option, with no increase in rent. When can I sign a lease?"

"I'll have it for you tomorrow."

Candice and I arranged to have our clothes and other necessary belongings moved to New York.

We started making phone calls and arranging speaking engagements to raise money for the redevelopment of the Sergeant Joseph L. Moskowitz Memorial Playground.

I was happy to be doing something useful again as boredom, retirement and watching my friends die off didn't agree with me. Now preserving the memory of a wonderful human being was my highest priority.

## Chapter XVI

## *Fundraising*

Candice, Eddie and I had divided up the list of potential donor contacts. She and I would contact half the list and Eddie the remainder.

Within thirty days, the three of us had scheduled numerous presentations, to take place over a four-month period, at various synagogues and Jewish organizations.

Initially, I read the speech Eddie had written, while Candice operated the slide projector showing the playground in its current blighted condition, and what it would look like refurbished, with the addition of a new team house.

The speech, with some modifications I made, gave the story of Joe Moskowitz's life—including the religious service he attended at the Dachau concentration camp and his subsequent untimely death, the history of the playground, and the civic good that could be accomplished upon its completion.

Following my presentation, I would entertain questions and after that refreshments were often served.

After one presentation, an elderly woman approached me. She was thin, with light brown hair, and seemed heavily burdened as she walked. She looked carefully into my eyes, as if to study them.

"I was in Auschwitz," she said. "You'll never know how bad it was."

I was stunned at first by her revelation. Then I replied, "I'll never forget what it was like when I entered Dachau. I can only imagine what you had to live through."

As she walked away, my heart sank.

I asked another person at the meeting about the woman who was at Auschwitz.

I was told that she was a classically trained pianist. I surmised that she survived the war because the Nazis would segregate the musicians, who would perform for them, from the other inmates.

After several presentations, Candice complained that I spoke in a somber, uninteresting monotone. She said I would be more natural if I spoke without the benefit of a canned speech.

I suggested that during our next presentation, she should give the speech and I would operate the slide projector.

At our next event, Candice gave the talk. It was full of ardor and passion, and the assembled seemed more attentive to her words than mine. During her speech, I had trouble operating the slide projector. At first I had the slides in upside down. Then I had trouble focusing them. My futility produced a wave of snickering which rolled through the audience, as Candice stood waiting with exasperated impatience.

After two months of presentations, Candice and I met with Eddie. As we totaled the contributions and pledges, we realized we had surpassed the halfway point of our fundraising goal.

At that rate, by December 2000, we would reach our goal and the playground refurbishment and the construction of the team house could commence.

We felt that the construction and redevelopment would be completed by August 2001, and a ribbon-cutting ceremony could occur in September 2001, with a date to be named shortly.

As we left Eddie, he invited us to attend his Saturday morning Shabbat service. I looked at Candice who said we would soon attend.

That Friday night we had to briefly drop in at the apartment of Candice's recently divorced daughter, Diane. We were in her living room when the phone rang. She took the call in the kitchen. As Diane returned, her face was etched in frustration.

"What is it, Diane?" Candice asked.

"The sitter called to say she can't make it tonight, and my date will be here in less than an hour. It's probably too late for me to get another sitter. Can you and David stay with Rachel?"

"Certainly," Candice replied.

"Thanks, Mom, and thank you, David. I'm going to change. Rachel is at a friend's apartment down the hall and she'll be here any minute."

*The End of Hell*

As Diane began to change, there was a knock on the door.

"Who is it?" Candice asked.

"It's Rachel, Grandma."

As Candice opened the door, she gave Rachel a big hug.

"David and I are sitting for you tonight," Candice said.

"Good," replied Rachel.

"David," she continued, "are you going to marry my grandmother?"

I was taken aback by her question and didn't answer. Then she said, "I know of some older people who were recently married."

I said, in a humorous tone, "Are they happy?"

"I don't know," Rachel said.

Rachel asked me if she could sit on my lap.

"Rachel, for you anything," I replied.

As she sat on my lap, she said, "David, when you grew up in Baltimore, what was it like?"

"Well, it wasn't like today. There was no TV, computers, or Internet. We didn't even have cell phones."

Rachel, looking sad, said, "How did you live?"

"We managed. We went to school, played sports, went out, listened to music and enjoyed ourselves."

"What schools did you go to?"

"I went to City College, a high school in Baltimore, and then the University of Maryland."

"You went to college?"

"Well, I didn't always look like this."

"Did you finish?"

"No, after two years of school, I had to go into the Army."

"When you were young, what kind of music did you listen to?"

"There was a lot of 'big band' music. We had band leaders like Artie Shaw, Duke Ellington, Count Basie and Benny Goodman, the King of Swing."

"Why did the band leaders have such funny names?"

"I don't think those names were any funnier than Prince and Madonna."

"David, those names aren't funny."

"I see."

"What kind of songs did they play?"

"The bands played popular songs written by great composers like George and Ira Gershwin, Richard Rodgers and Lorenz Hart, and Irving Berlin."

"Can you sing me one of their songs?"

"Here are some lyrics from 'Our Love Is Here to Stay' by Gershwin.

"In time the Rockies may crumble, Gibraltar may tumble–they're only made of clay, but our love is here to stay."

"David, that was nice."

"Yeah, and you could even understand the words."

"Can you do another one?"

"Here's another Gershwin tune, 'But Not For Me.'

"They're writing songs of love, but not for me; A lucky star's above, but not for me. With love to lead the way, I've found more clouds of gray than any Russian play could guar-an-tee."

"David, can you get me some CD's?"

"You know, Rachel, when I grew up, we didn't have CD's, just records. But I'll bring you some CD's."

"Thank you, David."

"You're welcome, Rachel."

At that moment, Diane's date arrived and as I stood up, Diane introduced us. After Diane left, Rachel climbed back onto my lap.

"David, do you have a family?" Rachel asked.

"I have two sons, Matthew and Louis, and four grandchildren: Josh, Susan, Henry and Ilene."

"What do your grandchildren do?"

"Ilene is in graduate school. Josh recently graduated from law school and is an attorney. Henry is an accountant, and Susan works in advertising."

"Does Susan write those advertisements you hear on TV?"

"Yeah, and she also writes such beautiful poetry, she makes me want to be born again."

"Would you tell me one of her poems?"

"Let's see," I paused. "Okay. How about this one: 'A little girl's smile is so beautiful even when mild.

'A vision of joy, more profound than any grownup's toy.

'A lasting memory not soon to be forgotten. A ray of hope even when I mope.

'A future that burns bright because a lot of little girls' smiles shall serve as the world's guiding light.'"

"That was beautiful, can you remember another?"

"The next one she wrote when she was seventeen. It goes like this:

'A little boy's frown is nothing more than a smile turned upside down.

'When I see a boy's frown, it reminds me of a sad circus clown.

'Little boy, turn your lips up, and you'll remind me of a pup ready to wag his tail as he jumps up.

'So, little boy, wipe away that frown and be happy like a real circus clown.'"

"I loved that one too, David."

"I'll tell Susan you're her biggest fan. She is very shy about her poetry."

"She shouldn't be."

"I know."

"When will Susan be in town?"

"Why?"

"I'd like to meet her."

"I'll tell her."

"Also, tell Susan I'd like her to teach me to write poetry like that."

"Okay."

"Can you write poetry, David?"

"No."

"Try one, please."

"How about this: If you don't soon go to bed, your mother will get a gun and shoot me dead."

"David, you're being silly."

"Can I stay up a little longer? ... Please!"

Candice, who was watching a TV program as Rachel and I talked, said it was okay.

"When I was little," Rachel said, "my mother and father took me to see the University of Maryland play basketball at Madison Square Garden. We had good seats right behind their team bench. Their mascot, the Terrapin, came over to my seat and patted me on the head. Then he leaned over and I kissed him on the nose. Did you know his turtle suit was torn?"

"Maybe he needs a new dry cleaner."

"David, you're being silly."

"Who won the game?"

"Maryland. But their coach uses lots of cuss words."

"Do you use cuss words?"

"Once, and my mommy told me to stop."

"Where did you learn cuss words?"

"When my daddy and mommy lived together, they cussed at each other all the time. Since he moved out, I don't hear those words anymore."

"All right, Rachel," Candice said, "it's time for bed."

"Yes, Grandma."

Before she went to her room, Rachel said, "David, can I give you a good-night kiss?"

"Sure. Besides, as I've aged, women seem to find me more attractive."

"David," Rachel smiled, "you're being silly."

## Chapter XVII

## *Rachel and Me*

I suppose because her parents were divorced and a father figure was lacking at Rachel's house, she began to adopt me as a surrogate dad.

That was fine with me as I loved spending time with my grandchildren, especially when they were younger.

Rachel would often call Candice and me and we would make plans. Whether it was attending a Saturday morning Shabbat service at Eddie's synagogue in Brooklyn, or taking Rachel to the East Village so she could find poetry books, or buying her CD's of some of the music I listened to in my youth, we had become a threesome.

When we took the subway, I would tell Rachel to be on the lookout for the right train. I always carried a subway map and spoke to the person behind a glass window as to what train to take. Then, as we rode on the train, I would make sure the streets went in the proper order so as to verify we were going in the right direction. When Rachel noticed my concern, she said, "David, you're being silly," and she told me not to worry.

When we attended Shabbat services at Eddie's synagogue, Rachel was very comfortable in these surroundings.

Immediately prior to the end of the first service we attended, Rabbi Moskowitz asked the guests to introduce themselves.

I stood and said, "I'm David Kravitz and served in World War II with Rabbi Moskowitz's brother, Joe."

Candice next stood and said, "I'm Rabbi Moskowitz's sister."

Candice's granddaughter then stood and said, "I'm Rachel Smalkin from Manhattan. Rabbi Moskowitz is my uncle, and I hope to see more of him in the near future."

When she said that, an undercurrent of whispering swept through the congregation.

The service soon ended and we went to the social hall where the cantor made a broche over the bread and wine and lunch was served buffet style.

Candice, Rachel and I sat at a table with Rabbi Moskowitz, the cantor and other members of the congregation.

Rabbi Moskowitz asked me about retirement and the business I was in. I told him our enterprise was called Four Seasons Coats. "It was a business," I said, "begun by my grandfather and father, who started out as peddlers and worked their way up from the streets.

"But the industry was changing, production was moving off shore, and there was no one in the family who was in the business. So when a good offer came, I took it. It was a fair offer from the beginning, so we didn't haggle much over the price. Besides, I knew the buyer was responsible and I was comfortable with the transaction.

"Since the business has been acquired, all the production has been moved out of the country.

"As part of the transaction, I kept all our buildings. Now, at least once a month it seems, I get offers from apartment and/or condo developers.

"'Who'd want to live down there?' I ask myself. When I was young, everybody living downtown was killing themselves to be able to afford to move uptown. Now the children and grandchildren of the uptown generation are killing themselves to be able to move downtown."

At that moment, several congregants came to our table to greet the Rabbi and compliment him on his sermon.

Following that interruption, I asked Rabbi Moskowitz, "When Brooklyn was going through its lean times, how were you able to keep your congregation together?"

Before he could answer, Rachel, apparently bored by our conversation, saw a table occupied by children her age and walked over to it.

As she did, Rabbi Moskowitz said, "Even though a lot of our members moved away, they kept their memberships and as their children grew up, they joined. We worked hard to attract and retain members. We had a strong brother and sisterhood, a book club, and brought in speakers on a wide range of religious and secular topics. We also appealed to young people, singles and couples."

"I'm surprised you don't have a Little League team," I said, laughing.

"We couldn't find a manager," Rabbi Moskowitz said, smiling. "David, maybe you could come out of retirement and become the manager."

"Casey Stengel," I said, "managed when he was in his seventies."

"Casey Stengel is still a 'dirty word' in Brooklyn as are the New York Yankees, Yogi Berra and Mickey Mantle," replied the Rabbi.

"How about if we call the team, the B'nai Israel Giants?" I said.

"Giants is still a dirty word in Brooklyn, too."

"I know we can't call them the Yerushalayim Yankees. How about David's Dodgers?"

"Okay," said Rabbi Moskowitz.

"At least, I'll be understood better than Casey Stengel."

"David, the trick in life is if you can't be understood, say things in a way that people will think you're a genius; or, at the very least, sound like you know what you're talking about."

"I'll need practice in that."

"So do I," replied the Rabbi. But, he continued, "To be a rabbi today, you need a little bit of Casey Stengel in you."

As we were getting ready to leave, Candice and I walked over to where Rachel was sitting. She was in an animated conversation with some of the other children.

Though reluctant to leave, she soon joined us to say goodbye to her uncle and the cantor.

As we left Brooklyn by cab, we saw a number of Hassidic families.

Rachel said, "I don't think I would want to live like that."

We soon returned to Manhattan when Rachel said, "David and Grandma, when can we go out again?"

"Call me, Rachel," I said.

"I will," she replied.

## Chapter XVIII

## *Ground Breaking Preparations*

With the fundraising for the playground continuing on schedule, Candice and I met with Rabbi Eddie Moskowitz in early October. The three of us decided we could stage a ceremonial ground breaking for the team house and playground refurbishments by December 1, 2000. Invitations would be sent to local politicians from Brooklyn, representatives of New York's mayor's office, current and potential donors, and members of the media. Following that, we would have a reception at Rabbi Moskowitz's shul where lunch would be served. Actual construction would start immediately following the ceremony, and we felt the playground, with its completed team house, would be operational by September 2001.

For the next several weeks, Candice and I met regularly with Eddie to plan a ground-breaking program, compile invitation lists and even plans for the September 2001 "ribbon cutting" that would officially reopen the Sergeant Joseph L. Moskowitz Memorial Playground.

As she did during the major portion of the fundraising campaign, Candice threw herself into the planning and execution of the ground-breaking program by helping to compile guest lists and personally calling approximately one-hundred invitees and members of the media.

Ever since Candice became closer with her brother, Eddie, in the playground fundraising efforts, the emotional barrier that had separated them disappeared. As the family became reunited, I saw a sensitive side of Candice I never knew existed. It was as if she had removed a mask and became a loving, caring sister, mother and grandmother. She seemed happier than at anytime since I had met her some four years ago.

I, too, was much happier, being active in a worthwhile cause. Had anyone told me, following World War II, something like this could have happened, I would have said, "Impossible."

But here we were, working to redevelop a playground as family fractures were healing. I'm not the most sensitive guy on Earth, but I felt good as Candice spent time with Diane, Rachel and Eddie.

A few days prior to the ground breaking, Candice and I had a Thanksgiving dinner at Diane's apartment.

After we had finished our meals and sat in the living room, I turned on a football game.

"David," Rachel said, interrupting my interest in the game, "I've been listening to the CD's you bought me."

"Oh," I said, somewhat surprised.

"How do you like them?" I continued.

"I love them."

"Well I'll be," I replied.

"David, Grandma and Mom, would you like to hear me sing 'The Man I love?'"

I got up and said, "Ladies and gentlemen, here's what all of New York has long been clamoring for: Rachel Smalkin's version of 'The Man I Love.'

"Rachel, the stage is yours."

Rachel then proceeded to sing "The Man I Love" and followed it up with "Bess, You Is My Woman," from *Porgy and Bess*.

At first I found it amusing as she began to sing but soon noticed her beautiful voice coupled with a developing stage presence, both of which deeply impressed me. I looked at Candice in surprise and she stared at me with a smile that expressed a grandmother's unrestrained pride.

After she performed her two numbers, Rachel went into her bedroom and returned with some poems she was writing.

Rachel wanted to know when my granddaughter Susan was coming to town so she could show her the poems.

"When Susan is ready to come to New York," I said, "you'll be the first to know."

"Good," she said, "maybe she and I will have lunch together. David, you and Grandma can come, but mainly I want to speak with Susan."

"Your grandmother and I understand," I said.

"Speak for yourself," said Candice, laughing.

That Saturday, I, along with Candice, Rachel and Diane, attended a Shabbat service at Eddie's shul in Brooklyn.

Following the service, Eddie, Candice and I briefly discussed the final details of the ground breaking.

By early afternoon, we headed back to Manhattan, with the ground-breaking day beckoning. And that was something that Candice and I, as we sat in the cab, took immense satisfaction in.

## Chapter XIX

## *Ground Breaking*

At 11 a.m. on December 1, 2000, the ground-breaking ceremony for the refurbishment of, and construction of a team house at, the Sergeant Joseph L. Moskowitz Memorial Playground was scheduled. The program was to take approximately forty minutes and following it, a reception was to be held at B'nai Israel, the synagogue where Eddie was the rabbi. Candice was the leadoff speaker. As she ascended the podium, I saw her drop her prepared notes. As I rose from my chair to pick them up, Candice began speaking extemporaneously.

"Life is funny," she said. "I'm back in Brooklyn, a place where I tried to run away from some forty-seven years ago.

"I was ten-years old when my oldest brother, Sergeant Joseph L. Moskowitz, died in World War II. Joe was such a kind, caring and sensitive individual, it was hard for me to envision him as a combat soldier.

"Yet he was a winner of the Bronze Star and, according to all the personal accounts I've heard, a fierce fighter.

"When Joe died, a pall descended over my family.

"I remember I wanted to do everything I could to end the misery in my household so I went to see a local rabbi. I implored him to ask God to bring back Joe. I told him what my brother's death had done to my parents and family. Surely if God could part the waters of the Red Sea, He could bring back Joe.

"The rabbi told me, 'God's ways are often not understood. One day Joe may return in an image that may be hard for you to understand.'

"When I graduated high school, I moved to Manhattan, leaving behind the misery that Joe's death had caused my family.

"I reinvented myself, as they say. I attended college at night and eventually rose to become an associate editor for a publisher.

"I married and became part of what are called the 'Beautiful People' with its attendant trappings: a Manhattan co-op apartment, charity balls, weekends in the Hamptons, etc.

"To do so, I became estranged from my parents and surviving brother.

"Yet I clung to the hope of the rabbi's words, that 'one day Joe may return in an image that may be hard to understand.'

"Four years ago I met David Kravitz, the man seated directly to my right. He served in World War II with Joe. He was near him the day Joe was killed.

"I never knew this until I sat with David to give him emotional support as he taped his reminiscences from World War II for a Jewish war veterans' group. I was horror stricken as I heard him speak into the tape recorder of Joe's death.

"I couldn't stand it anymore and became hysterical.

"I remained silent about my relationship with Joe until I attended David's grandson's graduation from the Columbia University Law School.

"Following the graduation, we came to Brooklyn because David wanted to see Joe's family's residence. Much had changed following World War II, and the neighborhood had declined considerably from the time I grew up.

"After we saw the residence, we returned to the cab, and I gave the driver directions to where we are standing now.

"When David asked me how I knew about the existence of the playground, I said, 'Joe Moskowitz was my brother.'

"I learned—even at my advanced age—you can't run from problems, because they are like shadows. The harder you try to run from them, the more they follow until they catch up with you.

"When I ran from my problems, I began to substitute calculation for love and responsibility. Is this the right address, the right place to vacation, the right set of friends? Also, I was far from an ideal mother and grandmother.

"When the opportunity arose to participate in the fundraising for the playground restoration and construction, I threw myself into it, without hesitation or reservation. And in doing so, I drew closer to my family and found a happiness I never knew.

"Fortunately, my efforts, along with my brother, Eddie, and my significant other, David Kravitz, have borne fruit as we break ground today for a new team house and to restore a dilapidated playground, enabling my brother's memory to be preserved in a way he would have appreciated—serving others, serving his fellow man.

"So to the donors and potential donors here, we are still looking to raise monies to set up a sustaining maintenance fund and for hiring a playground supervisor.

"If any of you wish to give, your pledges and contributions are welcome.

"As I've tried to do what's right with my participation and donations, I've found tranquility and fulfillment.

"May you do the same.

"Thank you."

As Candice left the podium, Eddie and I gave her a hug.

"Before introducing me, Eddie gave those in attendance a moment to reflect upon Candice's words of confession and hope.

As I took the podium, I decided not to speak from my prepared notes either.

"When I joined in the fundraising campaign, I, along with Candice, began making presentations before potential donors," I said. "I would give a speech as Candice operated the slide projector, showing the current appearance of the playground and what it would look like after the improvements were completed.

"After my second speech, Candice said, 'You speak in an empty monotone. Let me give the speech and you operate the projector.'

"So we switched roles. When it was my turn to show the slides, I found I had them in upside down. Then when I corrected that, I had trouble focusing them.

"At that moment, I thought about my grandfather's words after I started in my family's coat-manufacturing business following World War II. 'Dummy,' he would say, in his Russian accent, 'maybe you should go back to college.'"

The audience laughed and the mood lightened considerably from the solemn atmosphere Candice's talk produced.

I continued: "I met Joe Moskowitz in England as we prepared for the D-Day invasion.

"As I served with him, I found him to be a person of immense sensitivity and hope. Even as the despair of war and combat hung over us, Joe always maintained his idealism and a belief in the innate goodness of people.

"When I think about Joe, I think about the words of Anne Frank: 'In spite of everything,' she wrote in her *Diary*, 'I still believe people are really good at heart.'"

I then paused for a moment to let the audience reflect upon those words.

## The End of Hell

I began speaking again: "I've never been closer to anyone than I was to Joe. Fear and combat will do that—make brothers of soldiers.

"And Joe and I were essentially joined at the hip.

"We were at the liberated Dachau concentration camp and had just finished a prayer service when Joe was killed by a sniper.

"Yet I'm haunted by the last words I said to him.

"Following the service, I said, 'Joe, I love you. If we get through the next remaining days, I hope I never see you again. Even though you are as close to me as anyone I've ever known, if I see you again, it will remind me of the hell we've been through, and I never want to be reminded of this again.'

"As I walked away from him, Joe said, 'No, David, this is the end of hell.'

"Then I heard rifle fire and hit the ground. When I got up, Joe lay still. He was dead, shot through the head.

"I told Joe's brother, Rabbi Eddie Moskowitz, seated directly to my left, about my final words to Joe.

"He said, 'Joe knew you didn't mean them, that you wanted to end your horrific experience and any memory of it.'

"And Rabbi Moskowitz was right.

"Joe knew, because Joe had the spirit to rise up when others couldn't or wouldn't. When another step seemed impossible, Joe could marshal his spirits to take it, while believing in the goodness of humanity.

"Again, when I think of Joe, I think of Anne Frank's words: 'In spite of everything, I still believe people are really good at heart.'

"So to our guests, donors and potential donors, help us preserve a memory and a spirit that few of us have and most of us can only envy.

"I thank you for attending this event and listening to me.

"Again, my most grateful thanks and loving wishes to all of you."

As I walked to my chair, Eddie and Candice embraced me. Tears rolled from my eyes as I thought about Joe and the improbable journey that brought me here.

Eddie was the final speaker and instead of tapping the audience's emotional chords because of Joe's short life, he spoke of what the playground would mean to the immediate environment.

Following the speeches, a ceremonial ground breaking was staged and Candice, Eddie and I, a Brooklyn councilman, and a representative from the Mayor of New York's office were pictured sticking shovels into the ground.

Then, transportation was provided to Eddie's synagogue for those who wished to attend the reception and luncheon. At this event, a model of the refurbished playground and new team house was on display.

During the luncheon, Eddie, Candice and I table-hopped and thanked our donors and potential donors.

*The End of Hell*

As the reception was about to conclude, Candice's daughter, Diane, and granddaughter, Rachel, approached me.

"David," Rachel asked me, "do you think my Uncle Joe is in Heaven?"

I thought for a moment and said, "Rachel, your Uncle Joe has a special place in Heaven."

## Chapter XX

## *Candice's Disappointment*

I told Rachel that my granddaughter Susan would be coming to New York with her boyfriend, Joel, the day after Christmas.

"What will they do in town?" asked Rachel.

"Oh, a little shopping, some shows, and possibly a museum or two."

"Anything else?"

"When she arrives, we'll all have lunch together."

"Good," replied Rachel. "I've been waiting for this."

The day Sue and Joel arrived, Candice, Rachel and I met them at a mid-town restaurant for lunch.

After some introductions and brief conversation, Rachel showed Sue a new poem she had written:

'If a dog is man's best friend, what must a cat be?

'A girl's feline friend, that's what she has to be.

'If I had a cat, I'd name her Sue, so she'd always remind me of you.

'Because without Sue, my poetry would be as sad as Billie Holiday's blues.'

When Sue read Rachel's poem, she encouraged her to keep writing and gave her a hug. Rachel said her mother helped her with the rhyme.

"It's still very good," Susan said.

After lunch, we walked to Rockefeller Center because Susan wanted to see the Christmas tree. When Candice expressed surprise that my granddaughter wanted to look at the tree, I said, "What, a Jew can't admire a beautiful Christmas tree!"

When Sue saw the tree, she was disappointed and said it wasn't as beautiful or as full as last year's.

Joel said, smiling, "Sue, do you think you'll survive?"

Susan returned the smile and said, "Yes, but I'll need a strong man to get me through this period."

"I've been lifting weights," replied Joel. "I may be equal to the task. Feel this muscle."

"Can I feel your muscle?" said Rachel.

"Yes, but not too hard, you may hurt my arm."

Candice said, shaking her head, "Another comedian."

I asked Joel how things are in "the accounting 'racket.'"

"You know what they say," he replied. "Generally Accepted Accounting Principles or GAAP rhymes with crap."

"Are more poets coming into the Kravitz family?" Candice quipped.

Joel smiled and Susan blushed.

Following that exchange, Joel and Susan went off on their own.

As Candice and I returned to our apartment, Rachel went to another room and read a book I had bought her.

I sat in the den with Candice and turned on the TV.

"David, I'd like to talk with you," said Candice.

"Okay."

"Don't you think we're ready for marriage."

"I'm not ready."

"Why?"

"Look, there is a ten-year age difference. The chances are I'll predecease you. I've invested a lot of time and money in estate planning for my children and grandchildren. After I'm gone, I don't want to leave problems. Frankly, I want to die in peace and rest in peace."

"Suppose your heirs fight among themselves?"

"That's their prerogative and that will be up to them. But my estate planning is clear as to who gets what."

"We could always sign a prenuptial agreement."

"Yes, but after I'm gone, a prenuptial agreement can mean different things to different people. I've been to court when suddenly a dog became a cat. I don't trust lawyers or judges."

"Do you trust me?"

"Yeah, I trust you. But I trust me more. I want to remove, to every extent possible, the ability of outsiders to amend or reinterpret my wishes after I'm gone."

"So your answer is final?"

"I think so. Look, I love you, Candice. You've filled a void in my life, and I hope I've done the same for you. We have a good life together. We're comparatively healthy, and we go and do together. We're very fortunate."

"Yes, but without marriage, I feel a void."

"I'm sorry you feel that way, but we have a loving relationship."

"So there's nothing more to talk about."

"Pretty much."

At that moment, Candice paused. Then she stormed out of the room, angry.

I followed her into the next room.

"Look, Candice," I said, "we're no longer kids. The world looks a lot different to me now than it did sixty years ago. My age of innocence has long since passed."

"David, we're not talking about innocence, we're talking about marriage. Marriage is what happens when two people love one another."

"If life were only so simple," I said.

## Chapter XXI

## *Preparing for the Future*

Candice was upset with me for the next several weeks but knew my decision about marriage was fairly certain. She didn't like my decision but accepted it grudgingly.

Still, she decided, as I did, to keep our relationship intact.

In planning our immediate future, I told her I'd like to divide time between New York and Baltimore and maybe spend the month of February in Florida because of the warm weather.

She was agreeable.

I still had my house in Baltimore and both of us decided to keep our residences in Florida, so, as they say, we would always have a roof over our heads.

I wanted to stay active in retirement and spoke to Eddie about assisting him at his synagogue.

"What are you good at?" he asked.

"Oh, I could prepare promotional material, assist in writing a newsletter and do follow-ups with prospective members who inquire about joining."

"The job is yours," he laughed.

I decided, while in New York, I could work for Eddie two to three days a week.

## The End of Hell

In July, Eddie, Candice and I met to discuss the program for the reopening of the Sergeant Joseph L. Moskowitz Memorial Playground.

He informed me that, in addition to the short speeches that would be given, the Mayor of New York would be there to cut the ribbon to reopen the facility. Also a plaque bearing a relief of Joe in a dress-Army uniform would be unveiled. It would have the words I said about him to Rabbi Jonathan Taub on my return to the States on board ship: "A good soldier and a better human being." When I heard those words, I grew wistful but as we kept discussing the program, my momentary sadness was relieved. Eddie said the plaque would also say Joe was a "winner of the Bronze Star." Following the ribbon cutting, lunch would be served in the new team house. Five weeks before the event, a save-the-date notice would be sent, and twenty-one days prior to the occasion, the invitations would be mailed. All major metropolitan media would be contacted via a press release, and follow-up calls would be made to the approximately two hundred invitees and selected members of the media.

All that remained was to pick the date. Several were discussed. Finally Candice, Eddie and I agreed on Tuesday, September 11, 2001.

"Hmm," I said, "9/11. It has a certain ring to it. People will remember that date."

## Chapter XXII

## *9/11*

After the invitations and press releases were sent and Candice and I made follow-up calls, we left for Baltimore, where we spent the balance of August and early September.

We arrived in New York on September 9 and rented a hotel room in the Tribeca section so we could be close to Brooklyn. Immediately after our arrival, we met Eddie to discuss the final details of the ribbon-cutting ceremony for the opening of the team house and the rededication of the Sergeant Joseph L. Moskowitz Memorial Playground.

At the meeting, I found everything to be in order and, apparently, there would be no last-minute glitches.

After the ribbon-cutting event, Candice and I would return to Baltimore, but planned to come back to New York to live in her co-op apartment starting in October, when her tenant's lease would expire.

On the morning of 9/11 at 8:15, she and I went downstairs for breakfast. As I walked into the hotel restaurant, I saw a figure who looked vaguely familiar. I walked over to get a closer look at a man seated at a table with a woman.

"Sol, is that you?" I said.

"David?" he replied.

"I can't believe it," I said. "What are you doing here?"

"I'm here to attend the playground dedication in Brooklyn."

"How did you find out about it?"

"My son, who lives in Short Hills, New Jersey, sent me a newspaper article. So my wife, Helene, and I came. Here's a check for you."

I looked at the check and said that's "very generous of you."

"I'm sorry," he said, "this is my wife, Helene."

"Hello, Helene, I'm David Kravitz. Sol and I served together during World War II."

"I gathered that and am pleased to meet you."

As I turned to ask Candice to come to the table, she was already walking towards us.

"Good," I said, "I won't have to yell across the room."

"Are you still yelling, David?" Sol asked.

"I haven't stopped since I made sergeant. I think yelling comes with the rank."

I introduced Candice to Sol and Helene.

"Candice," I said, "Sol Goldman was my company commander during World War II."

Then I continued, somewhat wistfully, "Joe Moskowitz was her brother."

"I'm sorry," he replied. "Joe was a good man. He was the only person I ever met who could maintain his idealism in spite of everything. I'm so gratified I can be part of this event and donate money to it."

"Thank you for those kind words," Candice said.

Sol and Helene invited Candice and me to sit at their table. We were soon seated and Sol said, "It's a small, small world after all."

"Yes," I replied, "and it's getting smaller all the time."

"Sol," I went on, "where do you and Helene live?"

"In Chicago," she said.

"And you?" he asked.

"I think Candice and I will divide time between New York and Baltimore, and maybe spend February in Boca Raton to escape the cold."

"So I assume you two are together," said Sol.

"Yes, Candice and I met in Florida after we lost our spouses."

"David," Sol said, "it looks like you robbed the cradle."

Candice blushed.

"Are you two married?" Sol inquired.

"No," Candice said sarcastically, "we live in sin."

"You and the rest of the world," said Helene.

"How did you find out about Joe being Candice's brother?" Sol asked.

"I was taping my remembrances from World War II for a Jewish war veterans' group when I began talking about Dachau.

"It was traumatic getting through the segment, so I called Candice, whom I wasn't seeing too much of at the time, for emotional support.

"She came over and listened as I got through the segment. Following the episode, she left my condo, hysterical.

"I didn't find out that Joe was her brother until we were in New York, attending my grandson's graduation from the Columbia University Law School.

"I remembered Joe's Brooklyn address and Candice, I and some members of my family took a cab to see it.

"After I saw the residence, Candice gave the cab driver directions. He followed her instructions and we came to the Sergeant Joseph L. Moskowitz Memorial Playground. It was in horrible condition. There were needles along a fence line. A basketball rim, held by some loose wires, hung from the base of the backboard. The paving was torn up on the basketball and handball courts. There was graffiti on a concrete wall, and sections of the fence were ripped apart.

"I asked Candice how she knew of the existence of the playground.

"'Joe Moskowitz was my brother,' she told me."

"There are a lot of eerie links in a random world," Sol interrupted.

I continued: "There was a sign about fundraising. I called the man whose number was on it.

"Candice and I met him the next day. We were soon directed to meet Eddie Moskowitz, Candice's brother and a rabbi in Brooklyn, about fundraising.

"So we hit the fundraising trail, and helped raise the money for the refurbishment of the playground and the addition of a team house."

"There are some remarkable coincidences in that story," said Helene. "Truth, as they say, is indeed stranger than fiction!"

"Sol," I said, "you'll meet Eddie today. He's the program's master of ceremonies."

"I'm looking forward to it," he replied.

"Eddie is a lot like his older brother Joe," I said. "He's got those special sensitivities."

"You know, I always wondered," Sol replied, "what would have happened had we had the service in the main square of Dachau as scheduled on Saturday instead of Sunday, when Joe was killed."

"I've often thought about that too," I said.

"Sometimes," Helene interrupted, "we try to find meaning in a series of events like that, but the more we think about them, the less we understand."

After a momentary silence brought on by our contemplation of Helene's words, it was time to change the subject.

"David," Sol said, "I take it you're retired."

"That's right."

"How are you keeping busy?"

"Lately with the fundraising campaign in New York. Before that, not too much in retirement in Florida. Oh, I was in a card game, but that only makes time pass. To tell you the truth, when I stay in New York in the future, I will assist Eddie with developing promotional material for his synagogue and help with membership recruitment and retention."

At that moment, several cell phones seemed to go off, almost in succession. But Sol, Helene, Candice and I were so engrossed in conversation, we ignored the spate of ringing.

"Did you ever try to get a job after you retired?" Sol asked me.

"Yes, I tried to get a job getting in the way."

"How much does that pay?" he asked.

"I don't know, I couldn't get an interview."

Suddenly, a woman rushed to a table next to ours and shrieked, "A second jet has flown into the World Trade Center. Both towers are now on fire."

I looked at Sol, Helene and Candice.

"It's got to be terrorism," I said, after gathering my thoughts. "The jets don't fly down there."

The four of us got up, paid our bills, and walked outside, where we could see the smoke billowing from the towering infernos.

"Let's walk closer to the site," I said, "so we can offer help to those in need."

"I'll go with you, David," Sol said.

Candice looked at Helene, who nodded and said, "We'll go with you too."

As we walked towards the site, I looked at Sol and thought about D-Day, June 6, 1944, when then-Lieutenant Goldman changed the order of exit from the landing craft because I had been jumped and beaten by the southerners in my company because I was a Jew who danced with a Negro woman. I knew I only survived because he had intervened to reverse the order.

I thought about Joe Moskowitz's words following the prayer service at Dachau, after I told him I never wanted to see him because of the hell we've been through.

"No, David," he told me, "this is the end of hell."

As I saw the smoke billow from the towers of the World Trade Center, I knew there would never be an end of hell.

We all knew, instinctively, that the playground rededication would be postponed on this day, 9/11. But I also knew that hell doesn't last forever, and it was only a matter of time before the playground dedication would be rescheduled, because the goodness that Joe Moskowitz demonstrated on earth had to be preserved, just as Hitler and the people who perpetrated the crimes at the World Trade Center had to be destroyed.

Because in a world of evil, there can be no Joe Moskowitzes. And that's something humanity has to prevent, no matter what the cost.

## About the Author

Mark Carp is the author of *The End of Hell*. He lives in Baltimore, Maryland, and holds a BS degree from the University of Maryland and an MS degree from The Johns Hopkins University. *The End of Hell* is his third novel. His first two novels were *Abraham: The Last Jew* and *The Extraordinary Times of Ordinary People*.

Printed in the United States
131589LV00001B/1-192/P